THe Fast AND THe Furriest

The Fast and the Furriest

Andy Behrens

SCHOLASTIC INC.

New York Toronto London Auckland
Sydney Mexico City New Delhi Hong Kong

ISBN 978-0-545-38537-4

12 11 10 9 8 7 6 5 4 3 2 1   11 12 13 14 15 16/0

Printed in the U.S.A.   40

First Scholastic printing, September 2011

For mary Feltes

1

Twelve-year-old Kevin Pugh stood on the pitcher's mound. He squeezed a large red ball. Perspiration had gathered in dark semicircles on his WYCR-TV T-shirt. The June sun seemed to be cooking him, like a bratwurst. Or an Italian sausage. Or a smoked cheddarwurst—he *really* missed those. For reasons unknown, his mom had switched to chicken sausage, which he violently disliked. He kept telling her that all encased meat is not the same, but she . . .

"Pull your shorts up, honey!"

Maggie Pugh's voice cut into the quiet of the infield.

Kevin glared at his mom, who waved from the glossy green-painted stands. Kevin tugged at his droopy cargo shorts and bounced the ball in the dirt.

The print below the manufacturer's logo read OFFI-CIAL KICKBALL OF WAKA, THE WORLD ADULT KICKBALL ASSOCIATION.

"Dorks," Kevin muttered to himself.

"Uhds *gug,* Gev!" snapped the second baseman through a giant wad of radioactive-looking neon green bubble gum. "Uhduh-booty!"

He glanced over his left shoulder. His sister, Izzy (short for Isabella, which no one called her, ever), was clapping her hands and hopping, a black ponytail bob-bing behind her. Lean and wiry, Izzy had an unusually steely glare for a ten-year-old. Izzy was a local Chicago Park District soccer legend, but her awe-inducing ath-leticism went well beyond soccer. Other than parents and a mailing address, Izzy and Kevin didn't have a ton in common. Kevin needed a moment to interpret her gum-impeded speech.

"Let's *go,* Kev! Attababy!" Izzy repeated, still inex-plicably clapping.

Kevin shook his sweat-soaked shirt lightly to fan himself. A goose in left field honked.

"Time!" called a booming voice behind him. "Time out!"

Kevin's shoulders tensed.

He heard his dad's footsteps approaching from the shortstop's position. Howie Pugh—former Chicago Bear, beloved WYCR football analyst, and local sports demigod—was perhaps the most competitive human to ever walk the earth. No, the most competitive creature of any kind—mammal, sea slug, potted plant, whatever—to ever walk the earth.

Kevin wiped sweat from his face with the back of his hand and turned slowly.

Howie wrapped an arm around Kevin, engulfing him.

"Get your head straight, Kev," he said gruffly. "It's the sixth inning. Bases loaded. Two out. The go-ahead run at home plate."

Kevin scuffed his right toe in the dirt. "Thanks for the breakdown, Dad. I was expecting a hopeful sports cliché. 'When your back is against the wall . . .'—that sort of thing."

"Not an appropriate time for the sarcasm, Kevin." Howie spat. "What's the matter with you?"

"Um . . . for one thing, it's like a million degrees," Kevin said, staring into his dad's eyes. "And if you haven't noticed, they are now intentionally kicking at me, because I *suck* at kickball and they know I won't catch the ball. I thought we established that during last summer's WYCR-WFRK Charity Challenge. If you don't remember, I think there's a DVD in the basement that documents—"

"Okay, all right," said Howie, pausing awkwardly. "Just try your best, Kev."

"I *am* trying, Dad," said Kevin.

"Okay, kid." More aggressive spitting. "Then let's talk strategy." Howie spun his son around to face the next WFRK kicker. "*That* is Bradley Ainsworth Jr., the eleven-year-old son of six-time local Emmy winner Brad Ainsworth."

Kevin stared toward home plate. Brad Ainsworth stood behind the hitting screen. A veteran sports-caster at local TV station WFRK, Brad looked like a carved pumpkin, with his orange-ish fake tan and eye black on his cheeks. He was quietly delivering instructions to the small, angry-looking boy standing in the batter's box (or rather, the kicker's box). The boy also wore eye black. He kicked up a small cloud of dirt, like a bull preparing to gore someone.

The Brads both glared at the pitcher's mound, tilting their heads at the same angle.

"Big leg on this Ainsworth kid," continued Howie. "His dad used to punt for Northwestern. We can't pitch to him."

"You want me to *walk* an eleven-year-old?" said Kevin. "With the bases loaded? Is it even possible to walk people in kickball?"

Howie gripped Kevin's shoulders, his mustache quivering.

"No Ainsworth is gonna beat us, Kev. Brad Senior's got the top-rated drive-time sports radio show in Chicago." Howie stared at Brad Junior. "Besides, we've got a lead, and the next two batters are ladies. Easy outs. Go get 'em, kid."

Howie slugged Kevin's shoulder. Kevin wobbled. Howie jogged back to his position, clapping enthusiastically as he went. Kevin bounced the ball in the dirt and looked at a smiling Brad Junior. He bounced the ball again.

"C'mon, Kev!" chirped Izzy. "Goo ohg-eez chugs."

Kevin translated faster this time. *You own these chumps!*

The chugs own me, Kevin thought.

Kevin stepped forward, the kickball swinging back in his right hand. He released it, aiming nowhere near the strike zone.

The ball, however, did not obey Kevin.

It rolled smoothly and cleanly toward home.

From somewhere between second and third base, he heard his dad mutter, "Oh, fer cripes' sake, Kev."

Just as the official kickball of WAKA arrived at home plate—in the fleeting millisecond before the kicker's right leg hammered it—Bradley flashed Kevin a vicious smile. And then Kevin heard a sound like an M80 exploding inside a coffee can. He had just enough time to emit a small, helpless gurgle as the kickball whistled through the air. Directly at his face.

THWUNNNNG!

Kevin flew backward limply, hitting the dirt with a thud.

Spectators gasped. The goose in left field honked again.

"Kevin! Ball! Run!" Maggie, Howie, and the Brads were all yelling at once.

Slightly dazed, Kevin saw the ball spinning against the blue sky straight above him, like a red clown nose. It had ricocheted off his forehead, straight into the air. WFRK runners were circling bases. But if Kevin could simply catch the ball, the inning would end. No runs would score. Brad Junior would be out. And Howie Pugh would be very pleased.

"Get it, Kev!" yelled Iz.

Kevin stretched his arms toward the sky, his head resting in the dirt, his eyes squinting in the sun. The ball approached quickly. Kevin's palms were up, his fingers spread. The kickball hit squarely in his hands . . .

. . . and fell right through them.

It hit Kevin in the face. Again. Then the ball skittered off toward second base.

Kevin closed his eyes. He heard the Brads snickering. People were running—some scoring, others trying to retrieve the ball. Kevin groaned.

Just stay down, he thought.

And then he realized the worst part wasn't the people laughing at him, or the score, or even the dull throb in his forehead.

They still only had two outs.

The inning wasn't even over.

2

Kevin lowered a bag of ice from his forehead. He stared across the kitchen table at his father, who was noisily slurping down a diet root beer. Howie did all things noisily.

"Good game," Howie said, smirking.

"Not an appropriate time for the sarcasm, Dad," replied Kevin.

"Actually," said Howie, "this is when sarcasm works—*after* the game."

Izzy was idly juggling a balled-up sock. "It's just too bad you didn't stay in, Kevin. We totally coulda won."

"I was wounded," said Kevin. "Had to come out."

Izzy threw her sock-ball at Kevin, who lunged out of the way.

"Where were *those* reflexes earlier, Kev?" Howie asked.

"Not funny," snapped Kevin, adjusting his bag of ice. "I could have been killed today. Or brain-damaged. I could be in a vegetative state right now because of kickball."

Howie rolled his eyes. "That was pretty impressive, actually, getting hit in the face twice by the same kick. Is there somebody at *Guinness Book* we could call?"

Izzy snorted, then attempted to stifle her laughter for Kevin's benefit. She had retrieved the sock-ball and was propelling it toward the screen door that led to the Pughs' backyard. It landed with a rattle against the aluminum frame.

"Anyway," said Kevin, "I'm done with kickball." He drummed his fingers on the textured glass of the kitchen table. "It's dangerous."

Howie leaned across the table. "Listen, anything's dangerous if you're not focused. You can hurt yourself picking your nose if you're not paying attention, Kev."

"This second grader Olivia got Pez stuck in her nose last year," offered Izzy, removing her gum. "I saw her in the nurse's office. They were totally digging in there with these giant tweezers."

"In any case, Kev," Howie went on, "I don't care that we lost the game."

Kevin rolled his eyes.

"Okay, a little. I care a little. But I was disappointed you weren't *competing*. You were sleepy out there."

"I was wounded! That ball was like a meteor—it was like getting hit in the face with a flaming rock from space," Kevin said. "After the impact, it said 'W-A-K-A' on my forehead."

"No it didn't," said Howie. "From where I stood—running after the ball while you were just laying there—it seemed like maybe you'd given up, Kev."

"That's what it looks like when I play sports, Dad. It looks like defeat. I stink."

"It kinda reminded me of when you were whacked in the face last summer," said Izzy. "At my soccer practice."

Kevin thought for a moment. He'd sat through many practices and had been hit by many balls.

"Oh," he finally said. "You mean Maddie Siegel's free kick? That was no big deal. More of a glancing blow."

"It looked bad," said Howie. "You seemed to suffer."

"Still can't believe you didn't duck, Kev," said Izzy. "That soccer ball was in the air a *loooong* time."

"I do not respond well to flying objects," he said, looking down. "Especially in sports situations."

"So you say, Kev." Howie stood, lifting his orange

and blue Chicago Bears T-shirt slightly to scratch the lower hemisphere of his round, hairy belly. Then he smiled. "But you're a Pugh. We just gotta find the spark."

"The *spark*?" asked Kevin.

Behind Howie, Izzy was standing on one foot, balancing the sock-ball on the other.

"Yup," said Kevin's dad. "The spark that ignites the fire that becomes the big screamin' nuclear inferno of athletic dominance." He swept behind Kevin and whacked his back. Kevin cringed in fake pain. "You're a Pugh!" Howie stepped toward the fridge.

Kevin fussed with the ice in the bag. "I tried to catch the ball," he mumbled.

"We shall speak no more of it," said Howie.

Kevin reapplied the ice, eyeing an extra-large family-size bag of Blazin' Cheese Curls on the countertop. He was in that middle place of hunger where the desire to snack and the desire to not move are equal. He wanted the cheese curls, but not so much that he was willing to get up. If they were within reach, though . . .

Kevin's mom swept into the kitchen with her BlackBerry pressed to her ear. Spotting an opportunity, Kevin muttered, "Mom, could you maybe gimme the chee—?"

Maggie casually tossed him the bag and flashed

him a quick grin. She tore through the kitchen in a blur, deftly avoiding Izzy's whizzing sock-ball. Maggie nodded while speaking on the phone, a habit Kevin had always considered a waste of energy.

"Yeah, yeah, yeah . . . ," she said. "Yup . . . He'll be there . . . Sure, he can wear a jersey. Home or away?"

She hung up and wrote *"6 p.m. @ Sports Hut, Tues"* on the dry-erase board that hung above a pile of soccer cleats and a nasty-smelling pair of Heelys (both Izzy's). Managing schedules—mostly Howie's—was basically a full-time job for Maggie Pugh. She examined Kevin's forehead, smoothed his hair, said, "Poor dear," and then left the room.

Kevin crunched his cheese curls and looked at the jam-packed board. Three of the columns—labeled *"Dad," "Mom,"* and *"Iz"*—were completely full. Under his name, Kevin saw a dentist appointment and a haircut, both two weeks from now.

"Looks like my schedule has been enhanced," said Howie, shaking his head and grinning. Kevin rolled his eyes again.

Howie Pugh loved—*loved*—being a former professional athlete generally, and an ex-Bear specifically. It meant adulation at random store appearances; it meant getting paid to discuss the Bears on TV; it meant that grown men nervously approached him for autographs in restaurants.

Howie had been a sometimes-starting linebacker who had lasted seven seasons, all with the Bears. He was beloved in Chicago. Howie was the last player in NFL history to have played every snap of a game, both offense and defense. This happened almost accidentally in his final season, after several Bears had been ejected during a late December game against the Vikings. After a staggering loss, Howie breathlessly told a TV reporter, "We might be last in the NFC, but we're first in *trying*. . . ." Then he wobbled, collapsed, and flopped to the turf with a sickening *oomph*. The camera zoomed in on his closed eyes and drooling mouth. That image— slobbering, unconscious Howie Pugh—was emblazoned on T-shirts throughout the city, beneath three words:

FIRST IN TRYING

It was an impossible legacy for Kevin to live up to. Howie idly brushed his walrus-like mustache and sighed, turning to Izzy. But she had escaped to the backyard, where she was robotically rifling soccer balls into the upper left corner of a practice net.

"That's my girl," said Howie, glancing out the window. "Always working. Always trying." He turned to face Kevin. "And that's my boy. Usually eating."

Kevin kept crunching.

"We'll make a mean lineman outta you, Kev," said Howie. "Or maybe a nose tackle—those guys are huge. Like three hundred forty, three hundred fifty."

Kevin glanced down the length of his flabby arms. He licked orange cheese powder from his fingertips, then looked toward his father.

"Mom says that you were chubby at my age, too. It's genetic."

"I was *not* chubby!" snapped Howie. "I was *husky*. They're completely different metabolic states. It's basic science."

Kevin shrugged.

"Anyway," continued his dad, "you've got a good base, but we should get you in the weight room. I could already bench-press 180 when I was your age. Think what you could do with a little training, Kev."

"Yeah," said Kevin, standing. "So that I can attain kickball glory and vanquish the Ainsworths."

Howie shook his head. "No, so that you can start feeling good about yourself."

Kevin dumped the half-melted ice into the sink.

"So *who* can start feeling good about me, Dad?"

Kevin opened the door to the basement and lumbered downstairs to watch TV, certain that he'd feel just fine about himself if he could manage to go the rest of his life without playing another game of kickball.

3

Nestled in a nest of Bears-themed blankets on the basement sofa, Cromwell Pugh looked like a dog-shaped throw pillow. Howie liked to say that the mutt was part beagle, part potato chip.

Kevin plopped down beside the dog, sinking into a well-worn cushion. He couldn't tell anymore if Cromwell smelled like the plaid couch or the couch smelled like Cromwell. The pair had morphed into one creature, really. One musty, doggish-smelling beast.

To say that Cromwell was lazy was an insult to dogs who were merely lazy. He was inert. Most of his experiences with motion ended in epic disaster. A yellow Lab had once rescued him from the surf at the doggie beach. He had passed out while chasing a squirrel. He failed obedience school—not for dis-obeying anyone, but because he could *only* sit and stay.

Kevin propped his feet up on the coffee table.

"It's really best you weren't there today, Cromwell," he said. "I sucked." Kevin sagged a bit lower on the plaid couch. "And it was hot enough to melt anything with fur."

Kevin grabbed the TV remote from atop a mound of gamer magazines and pointed it in the direction of an absurdly large wall-mounted TV.

Click.

". . . Nicholson has his opponent dazed, flat on the mat! Every fan of mixed martial arts knows *exactly* what that means!"

"Stepover toehold facelock. Duh," said Kevin, yawning and leaning against Cromwell. The dog lifted his head, blinked, and closed his eyes again.

Click.

". . . that is perhaps the most precise run that I've seen from any dog since I began broadcasting these competitions! This dog is a legend, Bill. An agility champion in the truest sense!"

Kevin laughed and nudged Cromwell. "Check this out, dude."

A small black terrier zoomed above the Animal Planet logo, almost too fast for the camera to keep up. It leapt over small white hurdles and large pools of water; it whipped around cones and hopped through tires. A flashing yellow graphic on the screen read SHASTA AND JODY, 00:40.008.

"Bill, that's a new course record here at the Purina Incredible Dog Challenge!" an excited, nasal voice was half screaming. "It's like there's every other dog in the world, and then there's her. Wow, Bill. Just . . . wow. The divine walk among us—on paws."

Kevin laughed.

"It's hard to believe that you and that dog are members of the same species, eh, Cromwell? That has got to be the craziest thing I've ever . . ."

But when Kevin glanced at Cromwell, the dog was sitting up on his overstuffed haunches, his fat belly spilling over them. His front legs were shaking in excitement. His round brown eyes blinked rapidly. He was actually . . . panting.

Kevin stared at his dog while his dog stared at the television.

"Cromwell?" Kevin poked the dog's belly. "Dogs aren't supposed to respond to TV. I've read this."

Cromwell, apparently, had not read this. Because he kept staring.

"Nah, there's no way . . . ," said Kevin. He snapped his fingers at Cromwell. The dog didn't flinch.

The Purina Challenge had gone to commercial. A

collie appeared on-screen, moving in slow motion across a field of grass, its tongue flapping. It leapt over a fallen tree, then stopped abruptly at the side of a lanky woman in a babushka. The dog sat attentively. The woman nodded. She looked like a movie pirate, Kevin thought. Cromwell tilted his head slightly as a narrator spoke: "Whether you're looking to train a champion or just trying to convince the family dog that shoes aren't chew toys, Paw Patch can help. We've been training Chicago's dogs for over . . ."

"Okay, that's enough," Kevin said, changing the channel.

Cromwell snapped his head toward his owner. It was the single fastest move the dog had ever attempted. Cromwell looked at Kevin for several seconds, then dipped his head, whined, and scraped the couch with his paws.

"Fine," said Kevin.

He switched back to Animal Planet. Cromwell whipped his head toward the screen. The commercial had ended, and highlights of the terrier and her trainer snaking through the cones were being replayed. Cromwell barked enthusiastically.

"Crom, you're freaking me out." Kevin patted his lap lightly. "C'mere, boy. Let's chill. We'll go get your squeaky duck. And maybe one of those gross dehydrated beef treats."

A strand of drool hung from Cromwell's mouth for a moment, then cascaded onto a couch pillow.

Kevin shut off the TV, hoping to release Cromwell from the bizarre hold of the Purina Challenge. Instead, the dog flew from the couch, raced to the TV, then whined and growled. He stopped, sniffed the air, and barked. Then Cromwell looked back at Kevin.

"No, Cromwell," Kevin explained. "Those dogs weren't *in* the TV. They were just, like, *on* TV. Just pictures, Cromwell. Little pictures that move."

Cromwell whined again.

"Tele-vi-sion," said Kevin slowly. "There are these little dot-things called pixels."

Cromwell wasn't listening. He tore off, a brown blur skittering across the tile floor.

"Cromwell!" yelped Kevin in a half-disciplinary, half-confused tone. "Careful, Cromwell!"

THWAAP!

The dog struck a leather ottoman, shook himself off, then kept running. He slithered between a floor lamp and a chair, then clipped a table leg, overturning a stack of CDs. He leapt over a rug, landed nose-first on the tile, slid, and crashed into the mini-fridge. Cromwell scampered away just before a pyramid of small glasses, multiple boxes of bacon-and-cheddar-flavored crackers, and two Mike Ditka collectible plates tumbled to the floor like lemmings. Then the fridge itself tipped forward and fell. The sound was spectacular.

Kevin curled into a ball on the couch and braced himself.

Cromwell joined him, whimpering.

"KEVIN!!!"

His mom and dad had yelled in unison, which rarely happened. Normally Howie handled the yelling. Kevin heard their footsteps and lifted his face toward the basement stairs.

"It wasn't me! It was totally Crom—" Kevin looked at the dog. Cromwell was panting. His tongue hung out. He looked winded yet enthused.

Cromwell woofed.

Howie stood at the foot of the stairs, his eyes sweeping across the tile. Broken glass and shards of pottery mixed with assorted flavors (mostly variations on a cheese theme) of snack chips. Cromwell hopped down to sniff the wreckage. Maggie, standing on the bottom step, peered over Howie's shoulder. She rolled her eyes.

"The Ditka plates," moaned Howie. "He was my old coach. Those were limited editions, Kev."

"I had no idea, Dad." Kevin paused. "I microwaved them a couple times, if that makes you feel better."

Howie's cheek twitched.

"Sorry," Kevin said meekly. "Cromwell was just horsing around."

Cromwell barked and licked the tile floor.

Maggie patted her husband's back. "I'm sure Kevin didn't mean to break anything. Maybe you should clean up the mess, Kevin," she said as she headed back upstairs. "But get your sneakers on, and make sure Cromwell doesn't step on any glass."

Howie plodded upstairs, muttering, and closed the basement door.

Kevin hopped off the couch. Cromwell padded after him.

"Horsing around?" Maggie stared at her son. "You two don't *horse*, Kev. You loaf. You're chronic loafers." She gently pushed Kevin's sweaty bangs from his forehead.

"There are many sides to us, Mom. Cromwell is a complex animal." Kevin wasn't even sure he believed himself. "For example, did you know that he is inspired by televised dog agility competitions? Because I just learned that."

They walked slowly upstairs together. Cromwell followed, almost sheepishly.

"What are you talking about?" asked Maggie, glancing out the window to where Izzy was practicing her pitch.

"I'm talkin' about Cromwell and dogs on TV," Kevin explained. "Some pooch on Animal Planet was running this crazy course and Crom just took off, like he was in the competition or something."

"Kevin," said Maggie, shaking her head. "Rough-housing in the basement with your dog is one thing, but trying to convince me that Cromwell watches television? Did he eat your homework, too?" She had already begun pecking at her BlackBerry by the time he reached the kitchen. "No more horsing around, please," she called back with mock firmness.

"Tell that to my dog," Kevin quietly muttered.

Cromwell stared up at Kevin.

"Crom, that was insane. You don't move that much in a week." The dog licked his hand. "I bet those Animal Planet dogs don't decimate *their* owners' basements."

Kevin scanned the kitchen for a broom.

All those wasted bacon crackers, he thought wistfully. He snapped back into action at the sound of his father yelling from the family room.

"Kevin, if there are any large pieces of the Ditka plates left—big, glueable pieces—don't throw those out, please."

"Right," said Kevin, smirking at the thought of his dad lovingly gluing together pieces of Mike Ditka.

He grabbed his high-tops from the shoe pile near the door and turned toward the basement steps.

Cromwell stood in his way, tail wagging. And he had a leash in his mouth.

"Cromwell," Kevin said softly, "what are you doing?"

Kevin and Cromwell looked at one another. Cromwell dropped the tattered blue leash on the floor.

"A *walk*?" stammered Kevin.

Izzy flung open the back door, hopped over Cromwell, and grabbed a greenish sports drink from atop the kitchen counter. The beverage looked like nuclear residue, Kevin thought. Izzy skipped off.

"Okay, something's wrong." Kevin bent down and began stroking the dog's head.

Cromwell nudged the leash with a white paw.

Kevin pushed the decaying leash aside with his foot and walked downstairs. "*I've* still gotta clean up the aftermath of your last exercise experiment."

Cromwell paced at the top of the steps while Kevin mopped and swept.

"My dog sleeps," Kevin said quietly as he brushed cracker debris into a dustpan. "And eats. And sleeps and eats." He dumped the last of the glass shards into a metal wastebasket. "He's not a walker."

Kevin tried to decide whether the dog had exercised more in the previous ten minutes than he had in his entire life.

"Woof!" Cromwell barked, nudging the leash with his black nose.

"Really?" Kevin asked. "Like, seriously?"

"Woof!" Cromwell answered.

Kevin climbed the stairs and picked up the ancient leash. Cromwell's nails clacked excitedly on the wood floor.

"Just around the block," he told the dog. "And let's not make a habit of this."

4

When Kevin rolled out of bed the following morning, Cromwell was waiting, the blue leash clamped in his mouth.

"Incredible," said Kevin groggily, shaking his head at his energetic dog.

The ringing phone that had woken Kevin was still ringing. Apparently no one else was going to pick it up.

"Hello?" he mumbled into the phone, resting his hand on Cromwell's soft head.

"Dude," said his friend, Zach Broder. "Get online! Let's play Madden. I kind of own the Patriots defense at this point, if I do say so myself."

Cromwell inched the leash closer to Kevin's feet with his nose.

"Can't right now. I have to walk Cromwell," Kevin replied.

There was silence on the other end of the line. And then an explosion of laughter.

"Okay, I'm gonna go," Kevin said.

Zach was still laughing as Kevin hung up.

Kevin shuffled downstairs. Cromwell dragged the leash behind him and dropped it at Kevin's feet. Kevin poured himself a bowl of cereal—a blend, actually. It was one-third Double Chocolate Puffs, one-third Cinnamon Frosted Crisps, and one-third Berry Marshmallow Monster Pops. The recipe had been developed over months of trial and error.

Cromwell made a low, restless *rrrrrr*-ing sound. Kevin looked at him sideways. They'd trudged at least two miles yesterday around Lincoln Square, the Pughs' North Side neighborhood. Exhausted, Kevin had finally called his mom to pick them up from Welles Park—a ninety-second ride from home. How could Cromwell be so eager to repeat that humiliation? But the dog was pawing at the sliding door.

"Okay," Kevin finally said to Cromwell, setting down his empty bowl. "We'll go out."

They stepped into the yard just as Zach was heading up the driveway. Kevin's best friend hopped off his bike, stumbled, then lurched forward as a tangle of controllers and cords flew from his unzipped backpack. Zach was always falling. He looked up at Kevin, who was being dragged forward by his dog.

"Graceful dismount," said Kevin.

"Thanks," said Zach. "I'm a raw talent. Um . . . what's that on the end of the leash there?"

Cromwell was pulling Kevin toward the Pughs' expansive backyard.

"It looks almost like Cromwell. Except it's moving. Which Cromwell doesn't do." Zach walked alongside them. "What's up, Cromwell? C-Money. C-Dog."

Kevin unhooked the leash and let the dog streak off into the grass.

"He's a freak." Kevin shook his head.

Cromwell jumped over a garden gnome. Then the sprinkler. Then he tried to vault a bag of soccer balls, but two paws didn't clear the top. He rolled over the bag; then the bag rolled over him; then Cromwell popped up and kept running.

"New dog food, dude?" Zach was mesmerized.

"Nope. You know those parent–slash–old people groups that say television will make your kids do insane things? Well, Cromwell saw some dog agility contest on TV, and now he's totally lost it," Kevin explained. "He thinks he's in the Olympics or something."

"Dog agility?" Zach asked suspiciously.

"It looks like putt-putt golf," said Kevin, "but with a stopwatch and no ball. And, you know, dogs."

Kevin leaned against the house as Cromwell ran in a wide loop. Zach stared at the dog. Cromwell stopped, looked toward Kevin, barked, then started running again.

"That little guy can *move*," said Zach. "Never woulda guessed it."

Cromwell's left front paw became briefly entangled in a garden hose, but he shook it free. Then he took a few slow, tentative steps toward a tire swing that hung from a maple tree near the back fence. He woofed at the tire. Then he looked at Kevin.

"No, I don't think so, Cromwell," Kevin warned. "It's, like, two feet off the ground. You'll never make it through—"

The dog was off, sprinting as hard as he could, his soft belly nearly scraping the ground. Cromwell hurdled a small flagstone wall, brushing past Maggie's perennials, then bounded toward the low-hanging tire.

"*Go*, Cromwell!" shouted Zach.

"*No*, Cromwell!" shouted Kevin.

The dog approached the swing, dipped his head, sprang upward off his paws, and flew—Cromwell Pugh, Earth's laziest dog, literally flew through the air. Quite gracefully, really . . . until his head collided with the tire with a deep, rubbery thud.

The collision knocked Cromwell onto his back. The tire wobbled.

"Ouch," said Kevin and Zach in unison, both cringing.

Kevin ran toward Cromwell. But before Kevin could help Cromwell back onto his paws, the dog had shaken off his failure and began galloping around the yard, his tongue hanging from the side of his mouth.

"Cromwell!" shouted Kevin. "Sit, boy!"

But there was no "sit" in Cromwell.

Instead, he picked up speed, cruising along the flower beds that ringed the yard, occasionally kicking up a little dirt.

"No, Cromwell!" said Kevin firmly, waving his arms. This couldn't be happening.

Zach cheered wildly.

The look in Cromwell's eyes was pure determination.

Kevin froze, stunned by the sight of his dog—his fat, lazy dog—running. And preparing to jump through the tire. Again. This time, Cromwell took off just a few inches closer to the tire. He ascended at a steeper angle, eyes wide, slobber trailing behind him. Kevin braced for the inevitable collision.

Cromwell flew. And flew. Higher . . .

His front paws stretched, his head up, his ears back . . .

He rose to the tire's hole . . .

Until he peaked and his ample belly sank into the swing.

Cromwell hung there, limp and helpless, like a

furry piñata. The swing rocked lightly. Cromwell's front paws dangled from one side of the tire, and his rear paws from the other. He was suspended above the ground, immobilized. Cromwell's tail wagged, and he was panting. He made a small whimpering sound.

Zach was whoo-hooing. He jogged to the swing, clapping as he moved across the grass.

"Okay, *that*"—he paused for dramatic effect—"was *awesome*."

"I'm leaving him here in the tire. It's the only safe place." Kevin said, stroking Cromwell's brown head.

Cromwell squirmed.

"Kev, I don't know what exactly has possessed your dog, but you've gotta let him try that again." Zach couldn't seem to stop bouncing around.

"Again?!" said Kevin. "I need to tranquilize him. Tie him to heavy objects. He's clearly not made for this."

Cromwell reached forward with his front paws, first with the right, then with the left, as though he were paddling.

Zach began petting the dog's rotund middle enthusiastically. "Such a good boy," he said. "Yes you are; yes, you're such a good boy; yes . . ."

This elicited more tail-wagging, and a series of satisfied barks.

"You totally have to get Cromwell in those contests, Kev."

This was the most serious Kevin had ever seen Zach in the entire time they'd known each other.

"You can't be ser—"

Kevin was interrupted by the back door slamming shut. He and Zach instinctively tried to shield Cromwell from view, spinning around to face whoever had exited the house.

"KEVIN!"

Howie stood on the back step, glaring.

"Hey, Dad. Didn't hear you, um . . . over there. Outside."

"Hey, Mr. P," said Zach meekly.

Howie stared, then gestured toward the plump brown dog in the swing.

"You begged us to get you a dog, Kev. *'I'll take such good care of him,'* you said." Howie used a girlish falsetto for his impression of a younger Kevin, which his son did not appreciate. *" 'I'll walk him, Dad. I'll feed him, Dad. I'll pick up the poop, Dad.'* I don't remember you saying anything about torturing him."

"First of all," said Kevin, "I do not talk like a lady Muppet. Secondly, I *have* done the walking and the feeding and the poop-picking-up. And thirdly . . ."

"We all know Cromwell doesn't go for walks," interrupted Howie.

". . . And *third*," continued Kevin, "we are not torturing Cromwell." He paused. "Cromwell likes it, don't

31

you, boy?" Kevin scratched his dog behind the ear. But Cromwell had fallen asleep, his paws drooping from either side of the tire, drool clinging to the rubber.

"Just get the dog outta the swing, Kev," said Howie. "And don't put him in there again. It's cruel."

"He jumped!" protested Kevin.

Howie stared at his son. Cromwell had begun to snore.

"Move it, Kev." Howie waved at them dismissively and stepped back inside the house.

Kevin and Zach pulled Cromwell from the swing, and Kevin hoisted the dog onto his shoulder. Cromwell grunted and snuffled loudly, but remained asleep. Kevin strained to hold him as they retreated down into the basement. He gingerly placed Cromwell on a recliner, next to a well-gnawed beef-flavored snack stick.

"Cromwell's gonna sleep for three days," said Kevin, wiping sweat from his face. "He's never moved like that. Not even in fear."

Zach removed a variety of gaming accessories from his backpack.

"You need to enter your dog in those contests," Zach said. "Seriously. He could get product endorsements and stuff."

"Zach," said Kevin, picking up a game controller, "this is just a phase. And even if it isn't a phase, there's no way I'm running around the ring with

Cromwell. Those dog handlers are freaks." Kevin rolled his eyes.

"First of all, it's not a phase. He's got skills. A little practice—the right diet and training regimen—and he could be as good as any TV dog. And you . . ." Zach paused. "Well, okay. We might need to find someone else to run with the dog. Someone a little peppier. Peppy ain't Kevin Pugh."

Kevin half slugged Zach's shoulder, sending his skinny friend toppling off the couch.

"*What?!*" Zach exclaimed. "There's no shame in it. It's not like jockeys own the horses. They're just little dudes who *ride* horses. I'm sure it's the same with agility contests. You're not a dog jockey."

"So who is?" snapped Kevin. "You?"

Zach placed Madden '08 in the console.

"Well, I am nimble. And I'm probably telegenic. But no," Zach said, returning to the couch. "We need someone who's excited to be out there. Someone who isn't afraid to play sidekick to a big personality like Cromwell. Because the dog's a star. Cromwell's got swagger. He looked so . . ."

". . . rabid? Psychotic?" Kevin offered.

Zach shook his head. "No, happy. He looked really happy."

Cromwell snorted in his sleep and Kevin wondered if he was dreaming of leaping through tires. Zach was right; he had looked happy.

"Game on," said Zach, snatching a controller.

Kevin settled deeper into the familiar comfort of the Cromwell-scented couch.

"Game on," he replied intently. Maybe Kevin couldn't chase Cromwell across the yard, but he could certainly hold his own on the football field. Well, the virtual football field, anyway.

5

After a day spent running spectacular plays in musty darkness, Kevin couldn't sleep. His digital clock read 2:12 a.m. Cromwell snoozed at the edge of the bed—the dog had basically been unconscious since his morning romp. A fan whirred, stirring the air in the room. It didn't really cool anything. Kevin stared up at the dark ceiling, then at his dog, then at his clock.

2:13 a.m.

He watched the silhouette of a tree branch moving just outside his window. It was a moonless night. He thought he heard a plane pass overhead. He distinctly heard his dog whimper at his feet.

2:14 a.m.

Kevin looked toward Cromwell.

"You did look happy, Crom," he said. "Totally crazy. But happy." Kevin rolled onto his side. "And I *did* promise to take care of you."

He continued staring at the lump of a mutt, who offered an occasional *hmph*.

Another minute passed. Kevin stood, wiped his eyes, and shuffled over to his computer. He jiggled the mouse and the computer whirred to life.

Kevin brought up his Web browser. A search for "dog agility" returned a varied collection of links. He clicked on the first one. Skimming the Web page quickly, he saw lists of rules, examples of obstacles, world record times. Along the side of the page, listings for professional dog agility trainers proclaimed them "World-Renowned!" and "Premier!"

"Dog agility professionals?" Kevin grimaced into the darkness. He moved his mouse up to the search field and typed in "dog agility Chicago."

Most of the entries led to dog trainers who said they were "in" Chicago, but meant the suburbs. And suburban trainers were definitely beyond Kevin's travel radius.

"What was the name of that place with the pirate chick . . . ?" Kevin said.

And then he saw it.

When the site loaded, an animated dog—similar to the collie in the commercial—flipped several times against a graphic of the city's skyline, leaving a trail of paw prints behind that spelled out PAW PATCH. The words faded as a rotating image of the gray-haired woman from the ad emerged. She wore a headscarf, baggy clothes, a vest, and giant hoop earrings. All she needed to be a fully accredited pirate was a parrot and a wooden leg. The woman stretched her thin arms wide and said—in a supremely creepy computer voice—"Welcome to Paw Patch. I am Elka."

A menu of options appeared beside Elka's left hand. The fingers wiggled.

"Whoa," said Kevin quietly. "Freak show."

He clicked through to the "Contact Us" page. Kevin noted that Paw Patch's address on Clark Street was, in fact, within ten blocks of his house.

"Hmm," he said. He tapped his desk lightly.

Kevin clicked "Send Message" and filled out the online form.

Your Name:	Kevin Pugh
Dog's Name:	Cromwell Pugh
Address:	505 W. Ellbogen St.
City:	Chicago
State:	IL
Zip:	60625
E-mail:	klpugh@skycast.net
Message:	My dog is interested in your agility programs. We have a limited budget. Can we watch a class or something? Thanks, Kevin.

Another click and the note went off to the Paw Patch proprietors, possibly to the creepy pirate herself. Kevin then fell back in his chair and yawned. He looked over at Cromwell, curled into a tight ball of brown and white fur, snoring softly.

"The things I do for you, Cromwell."

The clock read 2:37 a.m.

Kevin sleepily wheeled himself to the bedroom door in his rolling desk chair, wishing he could glide all the way to the kitchen. Instead, he slowly stood up and walked downstairs, occasionally disturbing one of the old house's floorboards. He flipped on the kitchen lights, poured a large serving of Peanut Butter S'more Crunch cereal into a bowl—he didn't have the energy for the three-cereal blend—and then filled the bowl with chocolate milk.

"Hello, my old friend," he said, greeting the snack with a smile.

Kevin snatched a serving spoon from a drawer, then carried the cereal back to his room, milk sloshing onto the floor as he climbed the stairs. He placed the bowl on his desk, lowered his face to the rim, and began to eat.

"Mmmm."

As he wiped chocolate milk from the corners of his mouth, a small pinging noise caught his attention. Kevin looked up at his computer screen. An icon was blinking in the lower right corner. He brought up his in-box.

From: elka.brandt@pawpatchchicago.com
Sent: Saturday, June 12, 2:38 AM
To: klpugh@skycast.net
Subject: Thank you for your interest in Paw Patch, Inc.

Dear Mr. Cromwell,

I salute you. Through either unfettered enthusiasm or subtle manipulation, you have led Kevin to Paw

Patch. A wise choice. You are a discerning pupil. Our summer session starts on Wednesday. You may visit us anytime. Full sessions are $200. I look forward to our meeting.

Also, if you would be so kind, please inform Kevin that his interest in my program is not optional.

Elka

Kevin had stopped chewing. Milk dripped from his chin onto the desk.

"Psyyy-cho," he said quietly. "Who e-mails a *dog* in the middle of the night?"

Kevin finished the cereal and pushed the empty bowl aside.

Then again, he thought, *who sends an e-mail on behalf of their dog in the middle of the night?*

Kevin shut down his computer and wheeled himself over to his bed. He pulled back the Bears comforter and crawled in.

Cromwell produced a sequence of low, dreamy woofs and squirmed a bit.

"We'll check her out, though, Crom." Kevin smiled at his dog. "*If* you're still possessed." Kevin yawned. "But it's probably just a phase."

6

After the initial late-night e-mail exchange, Elka continued to write...but only to Cromwell. She asked that he—the dog—relay messages to Kevin.

When the Wednesday in question arrived, Kevin buckled Cromwell into an old bike stroller and latched the contraption to his eighteen-speed. Kevin would have walked, but he was afraid he'd wear out Cromwell and render him completely unimpressive.

After picking up Zach, he, Kevin, and Cromwell rode to a rather industrial-looking stretch of North Clark Street, stopping halfway so that Kevin could get a snow cone and Mr. Pibb. Zach purchased a lime Push Pop and a Yoo-hoo. They arrived at Paw Patch just after ten a.m., sticky from Popsicle residue. The building's exterior didn't exactly suggest that there were happy, well-trained dogs within. It seemed more like a place where people sent their old machinery to be repaired. Or a place where prisoners were tortured. Either way, it didn't scream "cute, cuddly dogs inside."

But it was definitely the right place. There were black letters affixed to the building's metal door:

PAW PATCH, INC.
E. BRANDT, PROPRIETOR
EST. 1985

"Just as spooky as its owner, really," said Zach. "Maybe she does have a peg leg."

Kevin gulped. He was unusually nervous. He removed Cromwell from the stroller and dropped him onto the sidewalk. Cromwell wagged his tail, sniffed the air, and barked.

"Good boy," said Kevin.

Cromwell barked again.

Kevin locked up his bike to a nearby rack, then pushed hard on the building's front door. It creaked open reluctantly.

Cromwell shot inside like a hairy, overweight bullet, with Kevin chasing after him.

Kevin and Zach went down a narrow, dark hallway. Kevin smelled the distinct scent of dog, but didn't hear any barking. Cromwell sniffed excitedly at the dirty linoleum floor and pressed on. He dragged Kevin behind him and pawed at another metal door. Kevin slowly turned the knob.

A high-pitched, gleeful noise emerged from Cromwell's brown and white mouth.

"Whoa," said Zach quietly, looking around.

An enormous white room was lined with airplane-hangar-size windows. Fluorescent lights glowed at the top of forty-foot ceilings. Green AstroTurf covered the floor. It reminded Kevin a bit of a Bears practice facility that he'd once toured with his dad, except that no one was shouting obscenities at sulking athletes.

Instead, a row of dogs were sitting obediently in front of similarly obedient owners. Kevin's eyes stopped on an icy-looking woman in a steel gray business suit standing behind a pristinely groomed King Charles spaniel. Next to her, a woman in apple green overalls stood at attention, her shaggy golden retriever wearing a bandanna that matched her overalls. Everyone's eyes were open wide, but no one was looking at Kevin or Cromwell. Their gazes were fixed on the bizarre figure at the head of the class.

Elka Brandt stood in the center of the room on a low platform. She had on a headscarf with a wild print—a babushka, as Kevin's grandmother would have called it. She wore weathered military-style boots that approached her knees, khaki shorts, and many bracelets on her arms. Surrounding her were neatly sequenced obstacles: a seesaw, pylons, wooden hurdles, a windmill, a series of plastic rings much lower to the ground than the tire swing, a kiddie pool, a long nylon tube, and a ramp.

Cromwell whined anxiously. Kevin cleared his throat, but Elka spoke first.

"Hello, Cromwell." She squinted at the dog.

Cromwell whined louder and wagged his tail frantically.

"Um . . . hello," offered Kevin.

Elka smiled.

"You're late," she said. "This class begins promptly at ten o'clock."

"Sorry," Kevin said softly, wiping snow cone residue from his hand onto his shirt. "There was . . . um . . . I had to stop. And I'm just here to watch. We'll stay out of your way—"

But Cromwell was apparently not in a stay-out-of-the-way sort of mood. He lunged forward suddenly, which caused Kevin to drop the leash. Cromwell ran onto the green turf, up the ramp, through the kiddie pool, into the tube—which rolled no less than six feet with Cromwell inside—and then

44

hopped through the rings. The leash bounced behind him.

"Cromwell!" shouted a horrified Kevin.

Elka seemed undisturbed. The other dogs and their owners kept still. Eerily still. Statue-still. Cromwell woofed and ran for the seesaw. Elka watched from her platform with a bemused expression. Cromwell raced up the seesaw eagerly, but when it began to tip, he tried to stop. And he wasn't any good at stopping. He rolled off, landed on his back, and let out a small, frightened cry. Then he backed up against the slowly turning windmill. Having no miniature windmills in his natural environment, Cromwell was startled.

So startled, in fact, that he knocked the wooden structure over with his meaty behind, then ran for his owner.

Kevin raced toward the dog, but stepped on a tiny hurdle that cracked under his weight. His ankle rolled and he fell to the AstroTurf, where he emitted a helpless *"Waaaahh!"*

Cromwell climbed on top of him. The dog whined, then licked Kevin's face, then whined again.

Elka clapped lightly.

Kevin cleared his throat. A youngish guy with crispy hair and an oversized polo shirt did his best to hide a laugh, but couldn't quite manage to. Even his schnauzer seemed to be smiling. Zach's amusement was more obvious. He was laughing so hard, he wasn't making any real sounds.

Kevin turned to Elka and, not quite looking at her, said, "Um . . . very sorry." Every inch of him was producing cold, nervous sweat. The windmill lay on its back, its arms still slowly churning. "Totally, completely sorry. This is clearly not for us."

"Well, it's definitely for Cromwell," said Elka. "He was brilliant." She smiled and nodded at the dog. "You, Mr. Pugh, are a different story." Elka gave him a firm, disapproving glance and adjusted her babushka.

Kevin looked toward his dog—his energetic, ambitious dog—and realized that getting thwacked in the face by a kickball in front of his dad's coworkers wasn't actually his lowest moment. Being shown up by his blob of a dog was much, much worse.

"I could . . . um . . ." Kevin cleared his throat and rubbed his ankle. "I could clean up the mess over there."

"No, no," said Elka. "Mr. Brockman will restore the course." She shot a severe look at the curly-haired guy, who recoiled, then hurried onto the green turf to rearrange the obstacles.

"Are you injured?" Elka asked Kevin.

"No," Kevin said softly. "I don't think so." He placed Cromwell on the ground, then sheepishly stood up. He felt an urge to flee. "I suppose you wouldn't mind if we just, um . . ."

"If you stayed?" said Elka, locking eyes with him. "Please, gentlemen. I *insist* upon it." She clapped her hands once and smiled warmly at Cromwell.

"But do try not to hurt yourself, Mr. Pugh."

7

For the remainder of the class, Kevin maintained a tight, unrelenting death grip on his dog's leash. He was like a mountain climber holding a rope. Cromwell seemed spellbound by the parade of leaping dogs. Kevin was no less impressed, but he also felt anxious and humiliated. When the class ended—despite his amazement at the talents of the various humans and canines—Kevin and Zach bolted. He later e-mailed Elka, both to thank her and to repeat his apology. Elka replied (again to the dog) and complimented Cromwell on his effort.

In the days that followed, it became perfectly clear that Cromwell was obsessed with agility. It was not merely a phase, but an addiction. He dropped his leash at Kevin's feet constantly. He ran phantom courses in the backyard. He lodged himself in the tire swing daily. It was mid-June and oppressively hot, but not even a series of 100-degree days could stop the dog. At times, Kevin would simply sit in a lawn chair, spraying himself with the hose, while Cromwell made run after failed run at the tire swing. Zach accompanied them on what Kevin felt were murderously long walks. At Montrose Beach, Cromwell ran through obstacle courses that Kevin constructed from abandoned tin pails and shovels; in Horner Park, the dog routinely broke free of his leash and tore through picnics and volleyball games; on the lakefront path, he chased bikes and terrorized pigeons. (Or maybe he just amused them. Tough to tell with pigeons.) He was an entirely new—and an unrelentingly active— Cromwell Pugh.

Kevin knew that they should really commit to Paw Patch. If they were going to keep up the dog agility nonsense, Cromwell needed more direction than Kevin alone could provide. All that remained was to convince his parents, who, Kevin figured, had always wanted him to be sportier anyway.

But Howie was a skeptic.

"Okay, just so I'm clear," he said over breakfast on Sunday morning, "you want me and your mother to pay for a class for Cromwell . . ."

"And me," said Kevin. "I'm in the class, too."

"Sorry. And you," acknowledged his dad. "We pay for a class where Cromwell *and you* get trained. But it's not sit—stay—fetch—roll over training? Or clean-your-room training? It's jump-through-a-hoop-and-leap-over-tiny-fences training?"

Howie, chewing, stared at his son across a plate of waffles. Each square on each waffle was filled with an equal volume of syrup.

"Yup," Kevin said.

"Cromwell's not going to start fetching things, though?" Howie continued, a waffle fleck flying from his mouth. "This is like dog show training?"

"Um, no." Kevin cleared his throat. "No, we won't be competing or anything. But it would make Cromwell happier."

"He's been depressed?" Howie asked before putting a perfect square bite into his mouth.

Cromwell was sniffing the floor for breakfast droppings, wagging his tail and occasionally pouncing on a speck of something.

"Well, no. Not depressed. But he hasn't really moved for the last few years. Now he's like a brand-new dog." Kevin could sense that his argument was getting thinner.

"And without a single class." Howie spoke and chewed simultaneously. "Why can't you two just keep up the walks? Let the dog keep whackin' himself in the head with the tire in the backyard or whatever."

Kevin folded his arms across his Cubs jersey. "If Izzy wants to sign up for soccer in Malaysia, it's no problem. We'll get vaccinated against six diseases and book a flight. I want to sign up for dog training in Wrigleyville and you're like, 'No way.' "

"Listen, I didn't say 'No way.' " Howie paused. "You know I'm happy to pay for anything you're into—but *you,* not the dog." He speared a strawberry, swirled it in whipped cream, and then scooped up a waffle chunk and rammed the fork in his mouth. "And c'mon. You can't compare Cromwell jumping over stuff to Izzy's soccer."

"Why can't I?" Kevin insisted.

"Because soccer's a sport—not a particularly American sport, I'll grant you. It doesn't involve much scoring or violence," Kevin's dad continued. "But there is *some* scoring, and there's fake violence. More importantly, it has a ball."

Kevin's eyes widened. *"What?"*

"Soccer is played with a ball, Kevin," Howie explained. "All sports involve balls. They can be kicked or thrown, doesn't matter."

Kevin stared at his dad for a moment, dumbfounded.

"So," he said at last, "surfing is not a sport?"

"Negatory, Kev. It's an exhibition," Howie declared.

"How about fencing? Or bull-riding? Or ice-skating?"

"Nope, nope, and heck no. Ice-skating? C'mon, Kev. You're gonna make me ill over here." Kevin's dad made wet smacking sounds as he chewed.

"What about hockey?" Kevin asked. "That has a puck."

"Pucks are like the metric equivalent of balls. So yeah, that's a sport."

"How 'bout bingo? That involves balls."

Howie lifted his head from his plate and spoke deliberately, as though explaining a fine point of law. "While all sports involve balls," he said, "*not* all things involving balls are sports. Like with juggling and pinball and so forth. That's an important distinction."

Kevin pressed on, unsure why he was prolonging the argument. "What about fishing? That's on ESPN all the time."

"If one of the two sides doesn't know it's playing," said Howie, "then it's not a sport. And the fishes definitely don't know what's up. So no, not a sport." More chewing.

Kevin stared at his father's ruddy face. "So that's it?" he finally said. "No interest in classes for Cromwell?"

His dad shrugged. "You're not makin' a good case here, Kev."

"I've got twenty dollars from Grandma from my birthday. I can contribute."

"It's just that your history of follow-through is not

so great," said Howie, gesturing with his fork, yet not looking up from his plate. "I don't want Cromwell coming to me and whining that you gave up after a month."

"When's the last time I quit something?" Kevin demanded, ignoring the idea of Cromwell telling anyone anything—and even if he could talk, dogs were loyal. That was the point.

Howie put down his fork.

"When's the last time you *tried* something?"

Kevin stared at his dad.

"Well?" asked Howie, waving a forkless hand.

"I try things," muttered Kevin unconvincingly.

"Listen," said his dad, softening his tone. "In theory, I like the idea of you getting a little more activity. I really do. How 'bout we sign you up for a camp that involves actual human sports? Let's start there."

"But I thought we . . ."

"I made an appearance last Friday at the Scherzer High School football camp, and it would be *perfect* for you. I gave a nice little talk to the kids. They loved me."

"Um, Dad, I'd rather . . ."

"The campers were all geeked up. It was sweet. I'm sure we could get you in, and I think it's only two or three hundred bucks."

"But the agility class is just . . ."

"Great counselors, too. And it's close to home. You could bike."

Kevin fidgeted. He could feel things taking an unwanted turn.

"Really, that's not what . . ."

"Heck, sometimes you can even take the dog! Then everybody wins! The little guy can nap under the bleachers while you learn how to block the power sweep!"

"Dad, I don't think . . . um . . . block the wha—?"

Howie was animated, bouncing slightly in his chair. "I'll have your mother call the camp, get you registered!" He grinned at his son. "And if you stick with this thing, Kev, then we'll revisit the little show with Cromwell and the pinwheels and the hoops. If he's still interested."

"It's not really a show, exact—"

Howie stood, then swept around the table and gave Kevin a playful tap on the head.

"Gotta scoot, Kev."

The door slammed. Kevin stared down at Cromwell. The dog's face was covered in waffle bits.

"That seemed to go well," sighed Kevin. "I thought I held my ground nicely."

8

Kevin and his mom stood in line together at Carnival Foods. Maggie was purchasing cleaning products and frozen vegetables. Kevin was buying a bulk bag of gummy fish.

"So let's talk about you playing football at Scherzer," Maggie said in a voice that seemed unnecessarily loud.

Kevin lowered his head, but glanced toward the girl at the register. She was maybe sixteen—possibly seventeen, but no older. She wore sparkly earrings. Her name tag read ERIN.

"Paper or plastic?" asked Erin cheerily. She smiled at Maggie, then at Kevin.

He looked at his feet.

"Paper," said Maggie. "Thank you, dear."

Two teenage girls entered the checkout line with diet sodas in their hands. They had ankle tattoos, beach bags, nose rings, and oversized sunglasses. They were giggling.

"Your father mentioned that you and he discussed football camp," said Maggie, still in the crazy-loud voice. "Is that right, honey? Do you *want* to do football camp?"

No, he thought.

Erin scanned Kevin's fish.

"Well, I could," he said, still looking down.

"Don't let your father force you into anything that you'd rather not . . ."

"You want these now?" asked Erin happily, extending the fish toward Kevin.

"Um, no," he said. "Just in the bag is fine."

Kevin shuffled his feet. The beach girls placed their sodas on the conveyor. Their giggling had quieted. Maggie continued.

"Because if you want to play football, terrific. But if you want to spend the summer in the basement doing your, um . . . TV things with Zachary, then that's okay, too." Maggie slid her debit card, then tapped at the keypad. "Whatever makes you happy. Just give me a yes or no, Kevin."

Kevin's mom looked up, smiling.

Erin smiled.

The beach girls smiled.

No, thought Kevin.

"Yeah, sure," he said.

And so it came to pass that Kevin Pugh committed himself—insincerely, yet in the clearest possible terms—to football camp.

It began early on Monday morning. Howie wanted to drive his son to camp—he pleaded for the opportunity, in fact—but Kevin insisted that being dropped off by a local sports celebrity would draw unnecessary scrutiny and complicate his camp experience.

"I wouldn't even have to get outta the car!" said Howie.

"You *always* get out of your car when you think you'll be recognized!" said Kevin. "Everywhere. At tollbooths, in drive-thrus, every time you drop us off at school."

"It's true, hon," said Maggie. "You do like to mingle."

Howie shrugged, then stroked his mustache. "I can be anonymous."

"Dad, you *stink* at anonymity. Your car has six Bears decals and a license plate that says PUGH 55. The horn plays 'The Super Bowl Shuffle.' "

"I can remove some decals. They're magnetic."

Kevin eventually won the breakfast skirmish, but not until his mom argued forcibly on his behalf. It was perfectly clear that Howie enjoyed having a son who was engaged in something football-related. It was not so clear whether Howie was proud of his son or proud of himself.

"Okay, no pressure," said Kevin, trudging gloomily toward Scherzer on his first day of camp. Cromwell bounced at his side. "Nooooo pressure."

His feet scraped along the sidewalk as he moved. A pair of new cleats—a gift from Howie—hung over his shoulder. He spoke to his dog.

"Assurances have been made, Crom: no pads, no contact drills. Minimal chance of injury."

The dog picked up a small, leafy branch, gave it a shake, and then discarded it.

"And the camp is for ages eight to twelve. I'm told that I'll be a giant among boys." He kicked a rock. "As opposed to a girlish liability among boys, which is my traditional role in P.E."

Cromwell sniffed a fence, then a hydrant, then a series of flowering plants.

"It really might not be *that* bad," continued Kevin. "Football is full of jobs that don't require ball skills. Half the people on the field at any given time are just trying to get in someone else's way. That seems like something I could . . ."

Kevin turned a corner and the field at Scherzer High School came into view.

". . . do."

Several dozen boys were zipping passes to one another. A group of coach-like people stood in a semicircle, watching. They all wore T-shirts with a crimson "S" (for Scherzer) and a cartoon bison (the Scherzer mascot). Cones were set up in neat rows, and tires had been arranged in zigzag patterns. Kevin was certain that he was at least five minutes early, but he suddenly felt late and lost . . . and possibly like leaving.

Cromwell, apparently feeling none of Kevin's reluctance, broke free from Kevin's loose grip and shot forward.

"You'd think I'd learn," muttered Kevin, "but no."

He ditched his cleats and sprinted after the dog, not quite matching Cromwell's pace—the dog seemed to have gotten quicker as a result of all the recent activity. Cromwell scooted through a coach's legs, his leash trailing. Kevin veered around the Scherzer coaches, then ducked to avoid footballs in flight. Cromwell hopped into one of the tires, then sprung up and landed in another.

Kevin dove at the leash, snatched it with his right hand, and reeled in his dog. He briefly thought that the incident had been contained—after all, when Cromwell broke loose at Paw Patch, he had left a path of devastation behind him.

Then Kevin heard a coach's whistle. He quickly realized that balls were no longer flying through the air.

The only sound was the snickering of other campers. Kevin sat on a tire, faced the group, and offered a small wave. He was nearly out of breath after his short sprint. Cromwell barked, and Kevin pressed the dog's substantial rear to the ground and whispered, *"Sit!"*

Cromwell barked again.

"Nuh-uh," said a voice from the crowd of campers. "No . . . *way* . . ."

Brad Ainsworth Jr. stepped forward. He brushed a lock of blond hair away from his eyes as he spun a football in his left hand.

Sure, thought Kevin. *Of course.*

"Hey, Bra—" he began to say.

"That's Howie Pugh's kid!" exclaimed Brad Junior. "The kickball star!"

A group of boys laughed as if they'd been trained to do it on cue. They stood behind Brad Junior like backup dancers. Kevin had a brief flashback to the moment the kickball had ricocheted off his face, but this was interrupted by another high-pitched tweet from a coach's whistle.

"Bring it in, men!" called a dour middle-aged man. He had a Scherzer cap pulled low over his eyes. The whistle hung at the corner of his mouth.

As the various Scherzer-shirted campers snapped to attention and clustered around the coaches, Kevin stood up slowly and walked to a shaded bike rack, to which he attached Cromwell's leash. He pulled a bowl from his backpack and filled it from his water bottle.

"Don't budge, Crom."

Yet another whistle pierced the air.

"Hustle it up, new meat!" barked the coach, clearly at Kevin.

"Dear God," Kevin muttered, jogging toward the group.

"Hustle!" snapped the coach.

Kevin broke into a loping run and joined the group.

"Sir," he said tentatively, "I dropped my cleats over by . . ."

"Hustle!" repeated the coach. "No excuses!"

Kevin ran his fastest—which wasn't especially fast—and joined the outer fringe of the group of campers. He caught a glimpse of Brad Junior smirking.

When Kevin joined the flock, the coach addressed everyone.

"Gentlemen." The coach paused for dramatic effect, as though he were speaking to soldiers on the eve of battle. "Last week was for drills. You threw, you ran, you caught, you kicked. You've hit tackling sleds and you—well, *you* haven't done this stuff, new meat."

The coach looked at Kevin, his eyes narrow and his mouth set in a straight line.

"But you've got a football pedigree, so I'm sure you'll catch up." The coach winked; then his eyes swept over the group. "Anyway, last week was for drills, and now we're going to put that work to the test." He clapped his hands. "We're going to play some games."

The campers cheered. Kevin cringed. The coach continued.

"We've already divided you kids into teams—eight- and nine-year-olds, you'll go to the south practice field with Coach Gutierrez and Coach Kirkland. The rest of you will stick with us."

He blew the whistle and the smallest, least intimidating campers broke away with the youngest, least intimidating coaches. This left the older kids with the angry whistler and two assistants.

The head coach looked at the remaining campers, then balled his right hand into a fist and pounded the logo on his chest.

"I love our mascot," he declared. "Who here can tell me about bisons?"

The coach surveyed the faces before him, then focused on Kevin.

"New meat!"

Seriously, that's the name we're going with? thought Kevin.

"Yes, sir," he said.

"New meat, when I say 'bisons,' what do you think of?"

Kevin cleared his throat. The campers spun around to face him.

"Well, they're a herd animal, first of all," said Kevin, his voice barely audible. "And I'm pretty sure they're plant eaters. And they were hunted to near extinction. And actually, I'm pretty sure the plural of 'bison' is just 'bison.' There's no 's' at the end, but . . ."

"Well, I think of *toughness*!" said the coach.

"Right," said Kevin, nodding like a bobblehead. "Toughness, sir."

"I think of endurance and fearlessness and *toughness*." The whistler paused. "Gentlemen, in football and in life . . ."

The coach then drifted into a practiced speech that was clearly intended to be inspirational and fiery. Kevin found it crushingly dull. He turned inward, embarrassed and bored. After a few minutes of lecturing, the coach said something—Kevin missed the particulars—that caused the entire group to woof like dogs. Cromwell joined the chorus. Kevin did not.

"Okay, men, take a lap!" declared the coach.

Everyone dashed for the track that surrounded the main field at Scherzer. Kevin lagged behind . . . and never caught up. He finished dead last, approximately forty yards behind an asthmatic ten-year-old. This brought more unwelcome calls of "Hustle!" and "C'mon, new meat!" Sweat stung Kevin's eyes. He was breathing hard, but all he'd really done was run a warm-up lap (badly).

The campers were soon divided into their teams. An assistant coach draped his arm around Kevin as they crossed the field.

"Glad you joined us, Pugh. I'm Coach Zalenski. You can call me Coach Z—everyone does. And *that*"—he gestured toward the whistler—"is Coach Hayden Glussman, one of the most successful coaches in Public League football. You're not allowed to call him Coach G. No one does."

Coach Z extended his hand for a fist pound, and Kevin obliged.

"Sorry I blew that whole bison-are-tough thing."

"No problem, Pugh. You were very thorough in your response, I'll give you that."

"So we're playing games already?" asked Kevin. "I mean . . . it's my first day. And I was led to believe this was a no-contact sort of camp."

Coach Z eyed him suspiciously as they walked.

"I'm assuming you'd prefer to go full pads, full contact. But no, Pugh, we're not allowed to hit here. It's an insurance thing. We play flag football."

He handed Kevin a grimy belt that presumably used to be white, but had turned the exact color of chicken nuggets. Two long yellow strips were affixed to the belt with Velcro. These were the flags. Coach Z bent low and whispered in Kevin's ear.

"If a little incidental contact occurs, Pugh, we're not gonna call a penalty."

"You know," began Kevin, "I actually dropped my cleats over . . ."

But Coach Z had already sprinted off, and he'd swatted Kevin on the backside as he did. Butt-slapping was definitely *not* one of Kevin's favorite sports traditions.

Within minutes, and with zero instruction, Kevin was standing on the football field at Scherzer High School, preparing to play defense. Alex Cribbs, a sixth grader, was yelling at him.

"End, Pugh!" He motioned toward the ball.

"End what?" said Kevin, raising his hands. "I wasn't even doing any—"

"*Defensive* end, Pugh! Play defensive end—on the line! Over there!"

Alex shoved him to an appropriate spot, then drifted back several feet.

Kevin stood flat-footed while his teammates crouched, waiting for the play to begin. Coach Z clapped. Coach Glussman stood halfway up the bleachers, his arms folded across his chest. The whistle was in his mouth just in case someone needed to hustle.

Brad Ainsworth Jr. seemed to have command of the opposing team's offense. The team huddled around him, then clapped in unison, then approached the ball. Kevin's teammates all struck serious-looking football poses, some bent at the waist, others kneeling.

"Trips left, trips left!" screamed Alex. This startled Kevin. Alex raced over to the left side and continued to scream.

Brad Junior stood at quarterback, a few feet behind the ball.

"Down!" Alex yelled, although nothing happened.

"Set!" Still nothing.

Kevin stood there, half amused and half terrified. Everyone else on the defensive line squatted low.

"Lightning, lightning!"

But again, nothing happened. Brad eyed Kevin, then broke into a smile.

"Scram eight-five-eight!" barked Alex.

Still no movement.

"Pugh!" called Coach Z. *"Puuuuugh!"*

Kevin turned toward the sideline and saw the coach gesturing, but he had no idea what was being signaled.

"Hut, *hut!*" yelled Brad.

Suddenly everything moved—except Kevin. Linemen were rushing, receivers were sprinting, Alex was chasing, and Brad Junior was pitching the ball to a running back.

Or not.

"Fake!" screamed two of Kevin's teammates.

"Pugh!" screamed Coach Z.

Brad spun, the ball still in his hands, and sprinted in Kevin's direction.

"Move, Pugh!" implored Coach Z.

Kevin took a few choppy steps toward Brad Junior and noticed that his nemesis was still smiling. Briefly, Kevin became determined to catch him.

"Come here, you little weasel, Ainswo—!"

Brad made a subtle head fake toward the sideline, then planted his foot and cut toward the middle of the field. Kevin attempted to reverse course, but, cleatless and unskilled, he failed.

In fact, he failed fabulously.

Kevin's feet slid to the right while the rest of his body went left. He felt himself lose contact with the ground—perhaps for a second or more—before face-planting with a thud.

He heard teammates and opponents groan, either in disappointment or in sympathy.

When he lifted his head and finished spitting all the dirt and grass from his mouth, he saw Brad Junior in the distance, high-stepping into the end zone.

A whistle blew.

9

Zach, I'm not discussing it," snapped Kevin, speaking into the headset. "Ever." His thumbs pounded away at a controller. His face was scrunched into a wrinkled, angry knot.

Up arrow . . . "A" button . . . left arrow . . . "A" . . . right arrow . . . "B" . . .

"Dude, it couldn't have been that bad," said Zach.

Kevin adjusted the microphone on his headset and spoke to Zach as they gamed.

"It was beyond bad, and I'm not discussing it."

"What did you tell your parents?"

"That it was fine. And then I came down here. End of discussion."

On-screen, a running back juked, stiff-armed a lineman, then sprinted up the sideline. A fake announcer declared this a spectacular move.

"Man," Kevin said flatly, "where are your line-backers, Zach? What is this? Bring a safety up . . . do *something*. You can't stop my run game."

A defensive back veered onto the screen, finally taking down Kevin's ball carrier.

"DUDE!" exclaimed Zach, his voice exploding through the earpiece and causing Kevin to duck his head reflexively. "That was, like, a game-saving tackle right there. That's clutch."

"Sure," said Kevin. "Twenty yards later."

Kevin scrolled through new plays.

"You seem to know what you're doing in Madden," said Zach. "How difficult could the transition to real foot—"

"Zach!" snapped Kevin. "Which part of 'not discussing it ever' was unclear?"

"Okay then, friend. Soooorrr-ry."

Kevin chose a passing play.

"A" button . . . left arrow . . . "A" . . .

"What's Cromwell doin'?" asked Zach.

"He's doing as much to stop my powerhouse offense as you are, chump," said Kevin. "Which is to say, he's doing nothing."

"Whatever."

Kevin sipped an orange soda with his left hand, and kept his right on the controller.

"Actually," he said, "Cromwell is sitting here on the couch, staring at me. At least I think he's staring at me . . . I'm sort of afraid to check. We were supposed to have a long, obstacle-filled walk after football camp, but, well . . . things did not go well for me. Not that we're discussing it."

Cromwell's ear twitched. Kevin noticed the movement and glanced at the dog.

"Aaaarrgh!" Kevin exclaimed into the headset. "He's *definitely* staring at me. I just checked."

"A" button . . . right arrow . . . left arrow . . . "X" . . .

"You've done him wrong, dude," said Zach.

"Completion!" said Kevin. "And how 'bout you do a little more tackling and a little less judging?"

The game suddenly paused.

"Oh, come *on . . . ,"* began Kevin.

"First of all," said Zach, his voice raised, "that was hardly a judgment. It was more like a simple statement of fact. I think we both know that you've done him wrong."

"I haven't do—"

"You've done him wrong, Kev. C'mon. Don't embarrass yourself by arguing the point. I know it, the dog knows it, that dog pirate-lady knows it . . . it's well-known. You should totally be at Paw Patch, taking classes."

"But my dad said we could maybe do those classes if I tried the foot—"

"You *hate* real football! Clearly. The fact that you're

so skilled at video game football is just one of life's little ironies."

Kevin was silent, except for the tapping of his fingers on the armrest of the couch. He didn't look at his dog.

"Cromwell is a natural at that agility stuff, Kev," Zach continued. "He's like the LeBron James of, um . . . obstacle courses for dogs. He's got crazy game. You need to get Cromwell in those little races. He could totally win." Zach paused. "Dude, I bet he would get sponsors! He could wear little doggie sweaters with corporate logos! You'd be ri—"

"All right, your point is made. You win. I'm a terrible person. Cromwell is a victim of my self-defeating worldview. And I stink at football. Again: you win. Now can we please get back to the ga—?"

"*No!*" yelped Zach. Kevin cringed, pulling the earpiece away from his head. "No, I don't think we can get back just yet," said Zach. "This isn't about me winning." He paused. "It's about Cromwell."

Kevin sighed.

"I hear you."

Cromwell whined, then sunk his head into the couch.

"If I were you," said Zach, "I'd quit football. I'd

just sign up my pouty dog for agility classes. Elka said he was 'brilliant.' "

"Actually, she said *'breel-yoont.'* Like she was a vampire." Kevin glugged more orange soda.

"Get your dog in those classes, Kev," said Zach with unusual conviction. "He loved it."

"Maybe you've forgotten that he nearly destroyed the course. Not in a good way, as in, 'Oh, that was killer . . . you totally destroyed the course, bro.' But real destruction. Like with wrecking balls and heavy equipment."

The dog whined again, then seemed to harrumph.

"Sorry, Cromwell," said Kevin softly, reaching a hand out to stroke the dog's fur. But he still couldn't look at Cromwell.

Zach pressed on.

"Is this the relationship you want to have with your dog, Kevin? Really? Simmering guilt?"

They remained silent for several seconds.

"Um . . . *what?*" Kevin finally said. "Where'd you get *that*?"

"Heard it from a lady on *Tyra*. A family therapist. Very insightful."

"You watch *Ty*—"

"Just stop," said Zach. "It's possible that I've said too much."

Kevin sighed. "No," he said. "You're right." Kevin

turned to face Cromwell, who was, in fact, still looking up at him with deep, dark, sorrowful dog eyes. "Really, you're right. I should take those classes. It couldn't hurt. He's my best nonhuman friend, and he doesn't ask for much."

Another series of noises from Cromwell.

"There are, however, two problems," added Kevin.

"You're too lazy and TV-obsessed?"

"No, I don't really view that as a problem. It's more of a life choice."

"So what are the problems?" asked Zach.

Cromwell crept forward slightly on his paws.

"Number one, the agility classes conflict with the camp-that-must-not-be-named. I don't see any way around that."

"Dude, quit the camp."

"I can't quit. Because then my dad would call me a quitter—and he'd be right."

"No, it's not like that. This is a different sort of quitting, because you never actually wanted to do it. This is more like a belated no."

Kevin snorted. "There's a distinction that would be lost on Howie Pugh."

"Then fake an injury."

"Fake an injury that disqualifies me from football, but not dog agility?"

"Oh, right," groaned Zach. "Well, what's problem number two?"

"Money," said Kevin. "Last time I asked, I was shot down. I'm not interested in soliciting again. Dad wants Cromwell to, like, fetch things. Do tricks. Juggle stuff with his paws, bark on command . . . whatever it is trained dogs do. He didn't seem interested in agility contests. I don't think he sees the corporate sponsorship potential the way you do, Zach."

"I do have vision. Don't *you* have any money, dude?"

"I'm not exactly a saver. All birthday and holiday funds generally get spent at 7-Eleven. Or they're converted into gaming gear. You know this."

"Right . . . ," said Zach softly. "Maybe Elka offers scholarships?"

"For deserving but needy dogs, to dodge tiny windmills? Doubt it."

There was a lull, during which Kevin almost suggested they un-pause the game. But then Zach cleared his throat forcefully: "I'll pay for Cromwell's classes."

"With *what*?" Kevin blurted into the headset. "World of Warcraft gold? I don't think Elka is interested, frankly. She doesn't strike me as a particularly dedicated gamer."

"No, with my $3,806.16."

"Excuse me?"

"I have $3,806.16. Years of birthday money, change squirreled away, unused hot lunch funds." He paused. "It's in the bank. There's around fifteen hundred dollars in checking. The rest is a little less liquid, but it's earning interest."

"So you're a saver," said Kevin.

"When do I ever have to buy anything for myself? I'm indulged, dude. But yeah, I do tend to hoard things, and I'd like to help Cromwell."

"No, I can't let . . ." Kevin paused. "What the heck am I saying, of *course* I can let you pay. Heck, yeah." Kevin exhaled loudly. "If Cromwell ever takes classes, you're paying. Better you than Howie Pugh. Not sure when I could pay you back, though. Maybe after college."

"No need."

Kevin looked at Cromwell, who looked back at him.

"Sorry, Zach, bad connection. Cromwell and I thought we heard you say that I wouldn't have to pay you back." He jiggled the headset for effect. "You know these classes are a couple hundred bucks, right?"

"Right. I don't need to be paid back."

"Wait a sec. How can you be cheap and indulged

all your life, then just hand out large sums of money for dog tuition? That's really how you want to spend your freakishly large savings?"

"I'm *investing* in Cromwell, I'm not loaning. We talked about this in social studies."

"Cromwell does not pay dividends, Zach."

"I'm like his manager. No, I'm like the corporation—or the shareholders or whatever they are—that owns the Cubs. It's a long-term investment. I'll cover expenses, and I'll profit when Cromwell wins agility contests."

Kevin guffawed. Zach did not.

Cromwell perked up further, licking Kevin's hand.

"O-kaaaay," said Kevin. "Perhaps someday you'll buy a dog and his handler."

"We'll have to discuss your role, actually, Kev. I'm not seeing you as the han—"

"Oh, no. If you're supporting Cromwell financially, I'm in—and I mean, I'm really in. I'm subjecting myself to Elka. I'm the handler, period. There shall be no rift between me and Cromwell, even if we fail. And we're doomed to fail." He sipped more soda. "That would be the deal."

He heard Zach giggling.

"What?"

"Then I'd *own* you, dude. Like an employee. When

I say break time, it's break time. When I say work, you work."

Zach un-paused the game.

"Game on," he said.

Up arrow . . . "B" button . . . up arrow . . .

Kevin's receiver was chugging toward the end zone.

"Has your dad not found it odd that you're a total master at virtual football, and uninterested in actual football?"

"He can't tell one video game from another. They're all just a version of Mario to Howie Pugh."

"Good game, Mario."

Up arrow . . . "X" button . . . left arrow . . . up . . .

"I think you'll like working for me, Kev. You'll find that I'm a firm but generous employer, willing to accept your in—"

Kevin re-paused the game.

"I should take Cromwell for a walk—a brisk walk. A lazy man's run. Continue the informal training, just in case."

Zach sighed. "A nice step. But you should register Cromwell at Paw Patch, dude."

"I can't quit real football, Zach. No way. My dad would *destroy* me. And you don't own me yet."

Kevin removed the headset, set down the controller, and clapped his hands. Cromwell leapt—well, half leapt and half tumbled—from the couch.

Kevin shuffled toward the basement steps. Cromwell bounded up the stairs happily, if crazily.

"Dad would totally destroy me," Kevin repeated, looking at his dog, but maybe speaking to himself.

10

On Wednesday morning, Kevin accepted a ride to camp from his mom, though he refused to be transported in the heavily decorated Bears SUV. As they entered the circular drive at Scherzer's front entrance, Kevin said, "Don't even stop, Mom. Just slow the car down. I'll roll out."

"But I want to meet this coach of yours," his mom protested.

"I do *not* need my mom talking to my football coach."

"Oh, Kevin, it's totally normal. I'm an active, concerned parent. I want to . . ."

"Mom, you're Mrs. Howie Pugh. I'm the awkward son of Howie Pugh. There's waaaay too much Pughness already."

"Havali'l fahmwee pwy, Gev!" said Izzy from the back, through a mouthful of gum.

"I *do* have family pride, Iz!" said an exasperated Kevin. "I'm actually protecting the family name by keeping a low profile at camp." He turned to face her. "This might shock you, but I didn't exactly dominate on Monday."

She popped a bubble, then peeled a thin film of grape gum from her cheek.

"Gividime," she said.

"I'm *trying* to give it time. That's why I need Mom to chill."

"You kids put all this pressure on yourselves," said Maggie, shaking her head.

Izzy withdrew the wad of gum from her mouth. "I do not put pressure on myself," she said. "Pressure worries about *me*."

"Of course, dear," said Maggie. She stopped the car, but made no move to get out.

"Mom," said Kevin, "please swear that you won't introduce yourself to the coaches." He looked toward the field, where campers had begun to assemble. "You'll notice there are no other moms."

"Okay, Kevin. I swear that I won't be a responsible parent who gets to know the people who instruct her children." She gave him a serious look. "But just for you."

"Thanks, Mom," said Kevin, opening the door. He walked slowly toward the coaches.

"Get 'em, Kev!" shouted Izzy.

Kevin waved.

I'll be lucky to survive 'em, he thought.

Kevin walked on, his cleats clicking against the pavement—there was no way he was going to risk going cleatless again. He still held on to a dim hope that perhaps his lack of proper footwear was the reason he'd been so awful on Monday.

But it turned out that no, the footwear was not a major factor.

Today was equally bad.

During the warm-up lap, Kevin was again beaten by the asthmatic. His flag team lost 35–0 and 41–6, and most of the scoring plays seemed designed to expose his immobility, his ignorance, or both. Coach Z began the day enthusiastically, but by noon he was sullen, responding to campers only with grunts.

Friday was no picnic, either. Kevin's team lost 28–0 and 37–0, and the longer they played, the more Kevin loafed. Brad Junior unveiled a series of touchdown celebration dances. And it had been miserably hot all week. The heat had transformed Kevin into a sweat-soaked, sagging, un-fun kid by noon.

After the final whistle and the final lap, Kevin started plodding toward the bike rack to unhitch his dog. The rest of the campers walked off the field in groups, talking, high-fiving. Kevin walked off slowly, alone, muttering.

He felt a hand slap his back. This, he thought, must have been disgusting for the owner of the hand—Kevin's shirt was drenched.

"Hey, bro," said Brad Junior, jogging slowly and smirking blatantly. "Nice work today."

"Go away, little Brad," said Kevin. "Shoo."

Junior laughed. In the distance, so did his gaggle of friends.

"C'mon, Pugh. Don't be like that." He jogged a few more steps. "Say hi to your sister for me, okay? She's kind of a hottie."

He laughed again, as did his associates.

"Eww, little Brad," said Kevin. "And no."

He would have tried to chase down Junior for that comment, but a week of camp had proven definitively that Kevin couldn't catch him. Or anyone else.

"Pugh, how did your sister end up with all the athletic—"

"That's *enough*, Ainsworth," said Coach Z, who was suddenly walking behind Kevin. "We'll see you on Monday."

"But, coach, I was jus—"

"Good-bye, Ainsworth," said Coach Z sternly. Brad Junior jogged back to his friends.

"Thanks, Coach," Kevin said quietly.

"Sure, kid." Coach Z walked at Kevin's side, keeping his pace. "Hot out here, eh?"

Kevin shrugged. "Guess so," he said glumly.

"Can I ask you something, Pugh?"

Kevin shrugged again. "Okay."

"Why are you out here, exactly?"

Involuntarily, Kevin laughed. He quickly decided that was not an appropriate response.

"To, um . . . well, to learn certain fundamentals of, um . . . football."

"Really?" asked Coach Z. "Because your dog seems more interested in what we're doing than you do."

Kevin saw Cromwell sitting attentively in the shade. This time he said nothing in response. Coach Z continued.

"In real football, Pugh, people who lose focus can get hurt. You can't play with indifference."

"Yes, sir," said Kevin.

"So I've gotta ask it again, Pugh." The coach's voice was oddly serene. "Why are you out here?"

"My dad wants me out here," blurted Kevin.

He wasn't sure it was wise to admit that, but it certainly felt good.

"Ah," said Coach Z. "Well, yeah, you play like someone who's out here because he *has* to be, not because he wants to be."

"Ouch," said Kevin. "But yeah. Have to be. There's not much wanting."

Okay, that felt awesome, too, he thought.

"What are we gonna do about this, Pugh?"

"Well, my plan was to just suffer quietly. I can't quit." Kevin fanned himself with his shirt.

"Pugh, you're too young to spend all your time on things you don't like."

"I couldn't agree more," said Kevin.

Coach Z stopped walking.

"What are we going to do about this, Pugh?" Coach Z said again.

"Nothing," said Kevin flatly. "I'm not allowed to quit."

Coach Z sighed. "That's admirable," he said. "Really." He lifted his Scherzer cap, ran a hand through his thinning hair, and then repositioned the hat. "Can I just level with you, Pugh? Just straight-out level with you?"

"Okay," said Kevin.

"And you'll keep it between us?"

"Sure," replied Kevin.

"Pugh, I can't keep losing. Every day in these games it's the same thing: loss, loss, loss, loss, loss, loss. That's all we do. We lose. And when Coach Glussman is up there in the bleachers, he's not just evaluating you kids. He's evaluating *us,* his coaches.

And this is getting to be a problem, Pugh." He exhaled disgustedly. "I was a shoo-in to be Scherzer's offensive coordinator this year, until this camp started. And now we've scored exactly six points in six games—*six* games! And the teams are set for the duration of camp. And every kid has to play. And I'm stuck with . . ." He caught himself. "What I mean to say is that . . ."

". . . you're stuck with me."

Coach Z stared at Kevin. "More or less, yes. The losing has to stop."

"You could trade me to Coach Dombrowski's team."

"Oh, I've offered a trade," said Coach Z, shaking his head.

"You *did*?" asked Kevin, slightly offended in spite of the circumstances.

"Actually, it was more of a gift. I tried to package you with Alex."

"He's our best player!"

"Yeah, but you were kind of the sticking point in negotiations, Pugh."

Kevin shifted his feet. He looked down at his scuffed cleats, then back at his coach. "Sorry," he said, simply and pathetically.

"One of two things needs to happen, Pugh, because there are careers at stake." Coach Z placed his right hand on Kevin's shoulder. "Either you need to decide that you want this—that you actually *want* to be here, that you want to play well—or you need to tell your folks that football doesn't interest you at all."

"Well," said Kevin, "honestly, that first thing probably won't happen—I'm just being realistic, Coach Z. And the second thing *can't* happen. No way. There would be serious long-term repercussions."

His coach sighed. "Well," he finally said, "the good news, at least for me, is that Coach Glussman won't be here next week. He'll be at an offensive clinic at Eastern Alabama Polytechnic Institute. Very prestigious. So we've got one week to light a fire under you, Pugh." He smiled. "Or to convince you that your summer would be better spent elsewhere—and I can be very convincing when I need to be."

And with that, Coach Z walked toward the parking lot.

Kevin stood still for a moment, wondering what sort of convincing Coach Z had in mind.

11

Kevin spent the weekend nervously fretting. Monday was going to involve pain—potentially serious pain. And shame. And the pain and shame would be followed by total exhaustion; then the cycle would repeat. There were six weeks of camp remaining. Kevin needed to endure if there was any hope of getting his dad to agree to agility classes. Or maybe he just needed to endure in order to prove something to Howie Pugh.

Either way, endurance seemed key...and the thought made Kevin miserable.

On Saturday, he and Zach spent the day doing what Maggie called "TV things" and Kevin called "the only things I'm good at." Zach's parents took them to Taste of Chicago that night, and Kevin inhaled two turkey legs, a small order of paella, a large order of shrimp stir-fry, cheese fries, and, for dessert, frozen cheese-cake on a stick.

It was satisfying, but only in the moment. He was still dreading the week ahead.

On Sunday, Kevin decided to give Cromwell another workout. They began with a brisk run, but it soon became less than brisk, what with the 90-something-degree temperature.

And after six blocks, it became a walk . . .

Then a sticky, sluggish stroll . . .

And then Kevin and Cromwell reversed direction, slowed a little more, and plopped onto a bench at a bus stop. Cromwell panted. So did Kevin.

"This jogging stuff"—deep breath—"isn't so easy, boy." Kevin used his shirt to wipe sweat from his forehead. "At least in football"—deep breath—"I can take the occasional break."

A Chicago Transit Authority bus creaked to a stop and Kevin stood up. Passengers exited, looking not nearly as dreadful and tired as Kevin felt. A young blond woman with a yoga mat visibly recoiled when she brushed a little too close to him. He stood there, sweaty and still slightly breathless, fishing in the various pockets of his cargo shorts for cash. Something on the bus hissed. Cromwell kept panting.

"No dogs, kid," said the bus driver, a gruff woman who seemed, rather obviously, to be wearing a wig. The wig looked a lot like a yellow Pekinese.

"Oh, um . . . really? Because we're not going far, I . . ."

"No dogs. Unless it's a guide dog—which that ain't—there's no dogs on the bus."

"I have an astigmatism," said Kevin. "Very poor depth perception. Balls are always hit—"

The door shut and the bus pulled away. Kevin stood there, still absently patting his pockets.

"C'mon, Crom," he said. "Let's walk home. We can do this."

The dog barked.

"Well, okay, I know *you* can do it. I need a little pep talk sometimes."

They trudged home slowly.

Before going to bed that night, Kevin discovered that he—or rather, Cromwell—had received another e-mail from Elka Brandt.

From: elka.brandt@pawpatchchicago.com
Sent: Sunday, June 27, 5:38 PM
To: klpugh@skycast.net
Subject: Re: Thank you for your interest in Paw Patch, Inc.

Dear Cromwell,

Hope you are well, you marvelous creature. When you speak to Kevin, please suggest a dog snack with glucosamine and chondroitin. For healthier hips and joints.

Elka

"O-kaaaay," said Kevin, switching off his bedroom lights. "Thanks for the tip, dog e-mailer."

Cromwell whined.

"*Fine* . . . maybe I could check the ingredients on your treats, boy."

Kevin slept poorly that night. He dreamt that Coach Z was chasing him with weapons—knives, flaming arrows, catapults; he dreamt that Coach Z had captured Cromwell and forced him to run laps; he dreamt that Coach Z and Elka Brandt were battling, Jedi-style.

On Monday morning, Kevin's alarm viciously blared at 7:45 a.m. He winced, then mumbled, then whacked the clock repeatedly with his fist, then jerked the cord free of the wall socket and threw the clock into the hallway.

"Good morning, sunshine!" called his mom, who happened to be rushing past.

"Sorry, Mom," he managed, then yawned.

Kevin wiped the sleep from his eyes and prepared to meet his doom. Breakfast was unsatisfying, and so was pre-camp TV. Maggie offered to drive Kevin to Scherzer, but he declined.

Where I go now, he thought, *I must go alone.*

The walk to camp was long, slow, and gray. The skies were dark. Rain was expected, but sadly, not enough to cancel football. Cromwell stayed home, due to the weather and a grooming appointment. Kevin groaned when Scherzer field came into view. Brad Junior was already there, and already surrounded by his groupies.

Kevin looked at the ground and noticed that he'd forgotten his cleats.

"Gee," he said to himself. "Might not play my best today. Bummer."

With Coach Glussman out of town, the assistants collaborated on a short introductory talk, then made the campers run the usual lap—and that's when Coach Z's method of convincing Kevin to quit began to reveal itself.

"Pugh!" he yelled, just as Kevin was finishing. "You call that running?! Because I call it lollygagging!"

Kevin said nothing.

"Everyone take another lap!" continued Coach Z. "And please encourage Mr. Pugh to take this one seriously."

And so they all ran again.

When passing Kevin, most of the campers took the opportunity to insult him, and everyone urged him to hustle.

"Okay, men!" shouted Coach Dombrowski when Kevin finished the lap. "Let's play!"

Kevin began limping toward the field, completely drained.

"*Hustle,* Pugh!" yelled Coach Z.

Kevin broke into a trot. His coach soon ran alongside him.

"Have you had a chance to think about the conversation we had last week, Pugh?"

"Coach," said Kevin, "I still can't quit."

"Didn't I give you another option?"

"Well . . . I can't promise that I'll start enjoying myself, either. There's no fire."

The coach eyed him for a moment. "Then it's going to be a long summer for both of us, Pugh."

Coach Z sprinted ahead, blew a whistle—though not quite with the authority of Coach Glussman—and huddled quickly with Alex before the first game.

Alex walked away from their conversation nodding, then jogged over to Kevin.

"Coach wants you inside," he said.

"Um . . . okay," Kevin said. "It's supposed to rain today, so I guess that's cool. But I think the school is locked. Is there a key? What am I suppo—"

"No, Kev," said Alex. "On the line. On defense. He wants you on the inside of the line. Over the center."

"Right, sure." Kevin nodded. "Of course. Got it."

"Just do your best," said Alex.

Coach Z whistled again, and Kevin's team began to arrange itself on the field. A light rain began to fall. Alex stood a few steps behind Kevin at linebacker. Brad Junior huddled with his team just a few feet away, whispering instructions. Kevin stood directly over the ball. He stretched, then hopped in place. Kevin was jittery, despite the fact that no one expected him to do anything.

When the opposing team approached the line, Brad Junior winked at Kevin.

"Hey, Pugh," he chirped. "Did you say hey to your sister for me?"

Brad smiled.

"Sure did, champ," said Kevin. "She wanted me to tell you that you're a flaming bag of . . ."

"*Down!*" screamed Brad Junior, still smiling.

Kevin glared.

"*Set!*"

Brad's linemen were frozen in place, statue-still. None of them seemed particularly concerned with Kevin.

"*Hut . . .*"

Kevin continued his hopping. The rain fell harder.

"*Hut!*"

The ball was snapped to Brad, who darted to his right.

"Run! Run!" yelled Alex.

Kevin wasn't sure if that comment was directed at him or not, but he took off in pursuit of Brad just in case. None of the blockers chose to interfere with Kevin, which wasn't unusual.

Brad sprinted toward the sideline, but Alex cut him off. The quarterback turned upfield, flashed Kevin yet another smile, then danced around an attempted flag-pull . . . and scampered toward the end zone.

Several defensive players chased him, but Brad had a sizeable lead.

Well, that didn't take long, thought Kevin.

"Pugh!" screamed Coach Z from the sideline. "Don't give up on the play!"

Kevin did not.

He dipped his head and ran as hard as he could, although Brad was clearly pulling away. The quarterback crossed the goal line well of Kevin and the rest of the defense. Coach Z blew his whistle and raised his arms, signaling a touchdown. Only then did Kevin stop running.

Or rather, only then did he *try* to stop.

In the rain and without cleats, Kevin found that stopping himself was more difficult than stopping Brad. He slid along the wet grass like a skater on a sheet of ice. After three yards, he began to yell.

"AAAAAHH!"

He waved his arms, but nothing slowed his momentum.

"AAAAAAAAAHHHH!"

Brad Junior was directly in front of Kevin, but his back was turned. Brad was holding the ball aloft in the end zone, and seemed to be considering his touchdown dance options.

"AAAAAAAAAAHHHHH!"

Kevin's eyes widened as he neared Brad. He crossed the five-yard line . . . the four- . . . the three- . . .

"AAAAAAAAAAAAAAAHHHHHH!"

Brad spun around—not in reaction to the noise, but as part of the TD celebration—just as Kevin crossed the goal line.

In the milliseconds before they collided, Kevin saw Brad's expression change from delight to terror.

WHOOOMP!

Brad was like a mosquito on the windshield of a speeding truck. When the pair hit the ground, Kevin heard a small expulsion of air from Brad, followed by a crunch. Every player on the field gasped.

"Pugh!" yelled Coach Z, running toward the scene of the collision.

Brad's mouth moved, but no sound emerged at first. His nose was bleeding. He spat a tooth—or a significant piece of tooth—at Kevin.

Coach Z reached the fallen players.

"Puuu . . . !"

He looked at Brad.

". . . eeeeeeew. Yuck!"

Kevin picked himself up and brushed wet grass off his T-shirt.

"Um . . . my bad," he said.

Brad spat a little more. After several seconds, he sat up and regained his voice.

"Thtupid Pugh never thtopped! He thmashed right inta me!" Tears ran down Brad's face as he lisped. "I think I broke my nothe! And my mouth! I'm thpitting a tooth!"

Coach Z handed Brad a yellow penalty flag and told him to hold it to his nose.

"Try to relax, Ainsworth. It was an accident. Kevin tried to stop, but he was . . ."

"No I didn't," said Kevin flatly.

A powerful idea had hit him—nothing quite as powerful as what had just hit Brad, but powerful nonetheless.

"What?" asked Coach Z. "Kevin, I saw the whole thing. You tried to stop, but since it was raining, you . . ."

"No," said Kevin firmly. "I did *not* try to stop."

He and Coach Z exchanged a long look.

"I tried to hit Brad. And I did it."

Kevin pounded his chest, because that's something he'd seen NFL players do.

"Then that'th gotta be a penalty!" cried Brad, spitting a little more.

Coach Z continued to stare at Kevin, puzzled.

"Oh, it's more than a penalty, buddy," said Kevin. "I should probably get kicked out of camp. Expulsion is the only thing for a rule-breaker like me."

"Yeah!" yelled Brad, pressing the penalty flag to his face. *"Thuthpended!"*

"Yeah," said Coach Z softly, his eyes still locked on Kevin, clearly beginning to understand his plan. "Maybe this does call for discipline."

Kevin nodded at his coach.

"Dithipline!" wailed Brad. *"Dithipliiiiiiinnnne!"* Tears continued to flow.

The rain above slowed, and sunlight broke through the clouds.

12

When Kevin's parents were told of the incident, they clearly had a difficult time processing the details. That evening, Howie, Maggie, and Kevin sat around the kitchen table, listening to Coach Z on speakerphone.

"I'm sorry," said Kevin's mom, "but you're saying that Kevin—*my Kevin*—actually broke the nose of another boy?"

"And a tooth," said Kevin quietly.

"That's correct, Mrs. Pugh," said Coach Z.

"And it was the Ainsworth kid's nose, eh?" asked Howie, his eyebrows raised.

"Yes, sir," said Coach Z.

Howie nodded. Maggie swatted him on the arm.

"We're mortified, Coach," she said. "We don't

want *anyone's* nose broken. We feel terrible for poor Bradley."

"Of course, ma'am."

Howie studied his son from across the table.

That's right, Kevin thought. *I'm a baaaaad dude.*

Maggie continued.

"And your recommendation, Coach Zalenski, is that Kevin should not be allowed to return to camp?"

"For the safety of the other children," said Coach Z. "And so that he can learn that his actions will have consequences."

Kevin could barely hide his grin.

Maggie repeated Coach Z's words slowly.

"For . . . the . . . safety . . ."

". . . of the other children," said the coach. "That's right. He really needs to control that temper. Manage the competitive drive. Kevin's not tiny."

"No, he isn't," said Howie, a hint of a smile at the edges of his mouth.

"You'll be fully refunded, of course."

Despite several minutes of negotiation, Maggie couldn't get Kevin's punishment reduced. She offered multi-week suspensions and elaborate apologies. She offered Howie's unlimited camp services, too, but Coach Z wouldn't budge.

Well played sir, thought Kevin. *Hold your ground, Coach.*

Expulsion was the perfect resolution. And because of Howie's relative amazement at his son's new aggressiveness, Kevin escaped serious punishment at home. His parents called the Ainsworths to discuss the incident, and Kevin and Brad Junior were required to speak:

"Sorry about your nose, man."

Silence.

"And your tooth."

Continued silence.

"Brad?"

"It'th fine, Pugh. Hurtth a little, but I'm fine. You're not that tough."

"That's great, Brad. Again, very sorry."

"Thure thing, Pugh. Thay hi to your thithter, Ithy."

CLICK.

Kevin could forgive the sister comment that time, given the unfortunate state of Brad's face. After a lecture from Kevin's parents about learning to channel his emotions, the official period of punishment had ended.

Kevin retreated to the basement with Cromwell. He sat on the sofa, content. The dog curled into a ball of brown fur on Kevin's lap.

"Crom, my schedule has suddenly opened up."

The phone rang. Kevin saw Zach's number on the caller ID.

"Hey, Za—"

"DUDE!" yelled Zach, forcing Kevin to remove the receiver from his ear. "Is it true!? You broke Ainsworth!?"

"Well, it wasn't qui—"

"Because I heard you *obliterated* him!"

"Kind of, yeah," said Kevin. "It was ugly. But it wasn't intentional—there's no way I could ever catch that little guy on purpose. The silver lining here is that I'm kicked out of camp. I'm being punished—no football!"

"You must be heartbroken," said Zach.

"Indeed."

"But you're not grounded?"

"Nope, not grounded." Kevin smirked. "In fact, I think my dad was kinda impressed. Which is kind of psycho, but there it is."

"So this means . . ."

"Paw Patch gets the green light," said Kevin. "If you're still willing to sponsor us."

"Kev, I'm here for you. I've actually got a few different designs for the 'Team Cromwell' logo that I'd like to discuss. There's an apparel line that I've been sketching. And partnership opportunities with sports drinks. I've thought of an ad campaign that would be a great fit for a car manufa—"

"Okay," laughed Kevin. "Good to know we have your support."

"Oh, you've got it." Zach paused. "But you can't quit on me and Cromwell once we start this, Kevin. This *cannot* be like Boy Scouts. I got stuck in that little blue-suited cult for a whole year. Remember, when we sign up for agility classes, you'll be working . . ."

". . . I'll be working for Team Cromwell," Kevin said.

The dog grumbled in his sleep. Kevin scratched him lightly behind the ears.

"We're not running these agility classes by your parents, I assume?" asked Zach.

"Oh, no. Not yet, anyway. They might smell a setup. And I'm not sure I can sell them on the idea that you're paying for it."

Kevin couldn't wait for Wednesday morning, when they would return triumphantly to Elka's class. He considered e-mailing her that night, but the whole reply-to-dog aspect of her communication bothered him—or intimidated him, maybe. Coaches like Zalenski and Glussman didn't seem too frightening to Kevin. He'd encountered whistle-blowing hustle-mongers before. But he'd never been around anyone quite like Elka Brandt. She seemed slightly mystical.

It was two more nights of uneasy sleep for Kevin, but this had more to do with eagerness than dread. On Wednesday, he, Zach, and Cromwell arrived together at Paw Patch early, well before class, just to guarantee a solid second impression. They again used the bike stroller for the dog, which Cromwell seemed to enjoy. With football camp behind him, a serious weight had been lifted from Kevin's shoulders. Somehow, when they entered Elka's giant, AstroTurf-covered training facility, she didn't seem even remotely surprised to see them.

"Um . . . Ms. Brandt?" said Kevin tentatively.

Elka was arranging obstacles. Her back was turned to the door.

"Ms. Brandt, um . . . Cromwell and I would like to enroll in your class. If that's okay with you."

She placed a windmill on the ground, then stepped back to examine it. She said nothing.

"Dude, I don't think she can hear so well," Zach whispered to Kevin.

"Only my dogs and their handlers in the room, Zachary!" declared Elka, rattling the boys.

"B-but I'm the manager," Zach stammered.

"In this room, you are the annoyance." She turned to face him. "In my office, you wait. Go. Flee. Shoo, shoo."

She made a sweeping motion with her left hand.

"So can we still enroll, Ms. Brandt?" asked Kevin.

"Mr. Pugh," began Elka, "you may indeed. But you are woefully behind, I'm afraid. You're quite fortunate that your dog has a proper attitude."

She smiled at Cromwell. He sat attentively.

"Zachary, really, you may now leave."

"But I'd just like to . . ."

"*Leave*, Zachary."

Kevin motioned toward the door with his eyes. Zach left, but not without a clear display of reluctance.

"I'm financing this operation," he mumbled.

Elka shut the door behind him, then faced Kevin.

"Why, may I ask, are you here, Mr. Pugh?" She looked at Kevin skeptically. "Do *you* wish to be here?"

"Yes," he said as firmly as he could, nodding his head. Then he added, "People seem to ask me that question a lot. I must give off a vibe."

"Indeed you do," said Elka. She stared at him, then Cromwell, then back at Kevin. "We have a great deal of work to do, Mr. Pugh."

He nodded again.

"And I do mean *we*—Cromwell, me, and you. If you're going to train with him, you must train with his passion."

Cromwell barked, then whined anxiously, then pawed at the turf.

"As you can see," said Elka, "he is rather eager."

13

While·Cromwell was certainly eager, he was also not, in the strictest sense, good at jumping over things. Or avoiding contact with them. These were not ideal traits for an agility champion. Two weeks earlier, during their first visit to Paw Patch, those shortcomings were made painfully clear. This Wednesday, in their debut as paying students, it was just more of the same. Certain obstacles were toppled, while others were broken. Cromwell left a path of destruction wherever he went. They were no better in Friday's class, either. They badly damaged a windmill, and slightly damaged a Shetland sheepdog and a shih-poo.

Yet Elka seemed unbothered.

Cromwell could not have been happier.

Dog agility frustrated Kevin in ways that football camp did not—at Paw Patch, he actively wanted to succeed. At Scherzer, he'd just wanted to make it till noon, then leave.

As Elka's class filed out of the training room after their Friday session, Kevin asked if he and Cromwell could run through the agility course just once more.

She swept her hand out before her.

"The course is yours, Mr. Pugh."

Kevin had printed out a set of agility rules published online by some kennel club. He kept a folded copy in his pocket for easy retrieval and consultation. Kevin had committed the basics to memory, and he tried to visualize the words as he positioned a bouncing Cromwell at the course's starting line.

"Okay, Crom, let's try this one more time. When I say . . ."

Cromwell shot forward, a brown ball of furious movement.

". . . 'go,' " sighed Kevin, chasing after him.

The A-frame ramp shall have an over-all length of 9 feet and a width not exceeding 4 feet. The A-frame will have an angle of 104 degrees. Dogs must ascend the ramp, cross, and descend.

Cromwell jumped past the contact zone, rolled off the ramp, and scrambled to remount the obstacle. His paws churned wildly as he neared the apex of the A-frame. When he hit the top, he fell into an uncontrollable slide and twirled off the downslope, landing with a heavy *fwump*.

> Hurdles shall be supported by 2 poles, not to exceed 48 inches in height. The jump height will be 22 inches, and the horizontal poles shall be 1¼ inches in diameter. All hurdles must be performed in sequence.

The dog lowered his head and sprang off his front paws, easily clearing the hurdle . . . except for his tail. It nicked the bar, sending it clattering to the Astro-Turf. Cromwell spun around, sniffed the pole, and then sprinted off.

> The pipe tunnel, typically a nylon cylinder supported by wire, will be 24 inches in diameter and shall be 10 to 20 feet in length. Exiting the entrance and/or entering the exit are considered penalties. Jumping over the tunnel is forbidden.

Cromwell flew into the yellow tube, and the apparatus immediately began to roll to its right. The dog scampered through, but not before the tunnel had shifted well off course, causing the dog to exit directly into a different set of hurdles. Cromwell scattered several plastic poles across the ground, frightening the dog.

"C'mon, boy!" yelled Kevin.

The dog's tongue flew to the side as he dashed ahead.

> There shall be a minimum of 10 and a maximum of 12 weave poles, each 3 feet high and 1 inch in diameter. They will be spaced 18 inches apart. Dogs must enter from the right side of the first pole, then alternate poles down the entire line.

Cromwell entered the poles from the left, skipped several, and flattened three.

> The table will be 16 inches in height, and have a surface that is 3 feet by 3 feet. Dogs must come to a position of rest for 5 seconds atop the table.

Cromwell chugged toward the table, heaved himself up, and then somersaulted across, landing on his rear.

"Crom, buddy, you've gotta sit up there on th—"

But Cromwell had popped up, wild-eyed, and sprinted off.

> The seesaw will be 12 feet in length
> and 1 foot wide. The contact zone will
> be 3 feet in length. The maximum
> height of the seesaw is not to exceed
> 27 inches. The plank must contact the
> ground before the dog dismounts
> the . . .

A startlingly loud high-pitched whistle pierced the air—it was really much louder and more shrill than anything Coach Glussman could have managed.

Just as Cromwell was coiling into a ball and preparing to leap onto the seesaw, he froze . . . and skidded underneath the apparatus.

Kevin froze, too, then looked down at his dog.

"Mr. Pugh," said Elka in a cold voice. "Would you and Cromwell please come to me, just for a moment?"

"Oh . . . ," Kevin managed, terrified. "S-sure."

Elka was standing on the low platform from which she preferred to address dogs and their handlers. Cromwell was panting contentedly beneath the seesaw.

"Sorry about the, um . . . the mess here with the poles and such," said Kevin. "I'll clean everything up, Ms. Brandt. Really. I'll put everything back the way . . ."

"Nonsense, Mr. Pugh. That is not a concern. These things are meant to be jostled. A neatly arranged course feels unused. It's sad. I prefer the clutter."

"Well," began Kevin, "I'm sorry about that little, um . . . well, the issue with Mrs. Schumacher's shih-poo today. Cromwell doesn't seem to judge the hoops so well—it's the wobbling, I think. We have this tire swing at home. There have been other incidents. And Tinkles is such a small dog that when Cromwell gets going, he just seems to real—"

"Mr. Pugh," said Elka, a look of exaggerated confusion on her face. "Why do you assume that I have gotten your attention so that I might reprimand you? We do all of our reprimanding during class."

"Well, it's just, um . . . that was quite a serious impact for Tinkles. I have some experience with those situations. And that was some noise she made. Not really a typical dog noise. More like a dolphin."

"The Schumacher shih-poo is fine, Mr. Pugh. She has proven her agility merit—and today she has demonstrated her resilience."

Elka stepped off the platform and bent low to pet

Cromwell, giving Kevin an excellent glimpse of the swirled, multicolored pattern on her babushka.

Each day, a different babushka. She must buy them in packs of eight, like underwear, Kevin thought. It occurred to him that her age was almost impossible to know—Elka could have been as old as his parents, or possibly his grandparents. The combination of the headscarf, the accent, the unusual fitness . . . Kevin really had no idea. She intimidated him quite a lot.

Some of this intimidation was because of her uncommon connection with dogs.

Elka scratched Cromwell behind the ear, then knelt beside him and cupped his head in her hands. She whispered something into his right ear—something that was apparently intensely private—and Cromwell made a sound that was part excited panting, part laughter. It was not a noise that anyone else had ever coaxed from him, including Kevin.

Elka then stood up abruptly. She was almost precisely Kevin's height.

"I swear," blurted Kevin, "Cromwell is working so hard. If we're not cut out for dog agility, then maybe . . ."

"Mr. Pugh!" she said again, sounding aghast. "Cromwell's effort is glorious. It's magnificent. To say that Cromwell 'works' is not sufficient." She knelt again, patting his head lightly. "I meant to compliment him."

"Oh," said Kevin. "Well, that's very nice of . . ."

"I am surprised to hear you question your place here, Mr. Pugh. Because your dog is most certainly cut out for this."

Kevin had no response to that, to the idea that his fat dog—who until a few weeks ago had actually been inert and unathletic—was now, according to an expert, built to do something sporty.

Elka stood up again and continued.

"I have observed, however, that the slightest misstep—such as the unfortunate shih-poo episode, for example—causes you, Mr. Pugh, to wilt."

"Wilt?" asked Kevin.

"Like a cut flower, Mr. Pugh."

Kevin's shoulders slumped, his feet turned inward, his hands retreated into his pockets. It's possible that's what Elka meant by *wilting*.

"It is important that you match your dog's effort."

"I tried to . . ."

"We've discussed the importance of this."

"It's just that we've only had, like, three lessons, and we've already broken pretty much every obstacle. And half the dogs."

"He doesn't see them," said Elka. "The obstacles. Cromwell does not see them."

"Well, that explains why he can't get out of their way."

"No, Mr. Pugh. I meant that Cromwell does not see this course—or his world—as a series of obstacles." She poked Kevin's arm, and not lightly. "He is not so easily deterred, your spectacular dog. Cromwell sees opportunity, not these little obstructions. If he cannot jump them, he will simply bounce off them and go." She made a scurrying motion with her hand.

Elka stared at Kevin with a look that he took for skepticism. "But you, Mr. Pugh . . . you *can* be stopped." She abruptly strode toward her door, pinching Kevin's upper arm between her thin fingers and dragging him along.

"I have things to show you," she said. Elka produced a hypnotic kind of jangling sound when she walked, like a human wind chime, a result of the interaction of various bracelets and necklaces and keys and probably, Kevin imagined, small metallic weapons. Useful for disciplining undercommitted students.

Cromwell trailed them happily. He leapt a small plastic hurdle.

Elka flung open her office door. Papers that had been stacked nearby whooshed out, multicolored Paw Patch fliers mostly, but also pages of handwritten loose-leaf notes. It was a room packed with stuff, and the stuff was only barely contained. Stuff teetered from shelves; it spilled off tables; it sat in impossible piles on the floor, and at impossible angles. And there were pictures. Elka jabbed a finger toward the far wall, which was entirely covered in dog photographs.

"You look at these, please," she said.

Kevin stepped over and between the various messes to reach the photos. Many had begun to curl and yellow with age. There was one of a very attentive-looking schnauzer standing beside a large trophy. A banner that was too long to fit in the image read 1989 OAK FOREST KENNEL CLUB CHAMP. There was a photo of a large-tongued sheepdog with its left front paw extended, Elka shaking it (she seemed to be much younger in the picture, though Kevin wasn't sure). There was an odd-looking dog, perhaps a Labradoodle, wearing three medals around its neck.

"These dogs," said Elka, "they have won things over the years—some of them have won many things."

"It's very impressi—"

"It's nothing, and certainly not impressive. Winning is incidental. The achievement is in the learning."

Kevin looked closely at the wall of photos. He noticed a large picture of a familiar-looking young girl and terrier. It was autographed *"Shasta & Jody, XOXO."*

"Hey, we've seen these two on TV," said Kevin. "They inspired Cromwell's love for dog agility. Did you train 'em?"

"No, Mr. Pugh, but I have witnessed their rise to greatness. They're local, you know. Cromwell has excellent taste."

"Hmm," Kevin said, eyeing the pair in the photo. Shasta and Jody wore matching bows.

"You know," said Elka, "Cromwell has more enthusiasm than any dog on my wall. Probably more than any ten dogs."

Because he's totally insane, thought Kevin.

"You will need to equal this enthusiasm, Mr. Pugh. Not so easy for you, I think." She somehow stepped across the messes between her and her desk, then sat atop it. "You two will participate in the Paw Patch Invitational here in two weeks, yes?"

"Against other dogs?" blurted Kevin. "And, um . . . their owners? In, like, an actual contest?"

"Mr. Pugh, you compete against the course, never the other dogs. But yes, there will be other dogs—and their owners—competing, too. This event will qualify one dog for the Midwest Kennel Club Championship, which is really quite prestigious. It's held here in Chicago, at one of the sporting arenas."

"Soldier Field?" asked Kevin.

"No," said Elka.

"The United Center?"

"Ah, that's the one." Elka nodded.

Sporting arenas, thought Kevin. *Who talks this way?*

115

"It will be very good for Cromwell to actually compete alongside other dogs at Paw Patch, I think. He can be as good as you allow him to be."

Kevin said nothing. His dog woofed.

"It is not important for him to win, Mr. Pugh." Elka smiled at the dog. "For Cromwell, just learning to wait his turn will be a rather large achievement."

Cromwell whined, then splayed his front paws outward, knocking over a pile of notebooks.

If we manage to not hurt anyone, that would be a big achievement, thought Kevin.

14

It was a very good thing that winning wasn't important. Because in their training runs during class the following week, Cromwell lost to everyone, including a deaf terrier with benign tumors on its rear paws.

"Splendid!" crowed Elka from her platform at the end of Cromwell's run on Wednesday afternoon. He had toppled or otherwise misused every obstacle on the course.

Elka seemed particularly pleased with two things: one, Cromwell did, in fact, manage to contain himself until he and Kevin were supposed to begin—"You may interpret this as a sign that Cromwell would like to do well," she said—and two, Kevin did not handle Cromwell halfheartedly.

Instead, he ran hard, directing his dog as best he could, almost exceeding Cromwell's wild abandon.

"You appeared almost determined, Mr. Pugh," said Elka.

He had been determined . . . not to look like an idiot. He was sure that he'd failed in that respect.

"Of course you were both technically *horrible*," continued Elka, her voice rising on the adjective, "but this is what we expect. This is only the second week. Some dogs, they take years . . . and still they're not so good." .

Cromwell had appeared to get lost in a long nylon tube, he missed or toppled most of the poles on what was supposed to be a weave, and his paws never made contact with any of the points he was supposed to touch along the course—these contact points were meant to be tests of discipline. Of which Cromwell seemed to have none. Kevin consistently positioned himself incorrectly and toppled one or two obstacles himself.

Classmates always nodded approvingly. A graying man named Mickael and his dog, a Chesapeake named Vladimir, delivered encouragement and sniffing. A middle-aged woman named Frances and her collie Willamina—this pair lent validity to the whole pets-look-like-their-owners thing—offered support to Kevin and to Cromwell, too.

Zach accompanied Kevin to each class, sitting just outside the training area. He cracked open the door occasionally and peeked inside. Elka must have noticed, though she allowed it. Zach was bubbling over with enthusiasm after the Wednesday session.

"That was excellent! Cromwell was a beast! A super-fast beast! He was total—"

"He was a spazzy goof," said Kevin. "And so was I."

Kevin shuffled along North Clark Street, past rock clubs and hot dog stands, Cromwell cheerfully wagging at his feet. Zach attempted progressively less-enthused words of encouragement, hoping to find something that Kevin would concur with.

"Well, as the investor behind all this," he said, "I think I got my money's worth. This was an important day for Team Cromwell."

"You're a nut," said Kevin dourly.

"I'm the CEO!" declared Zach. "The CEO can't be a nut. I have vision. And our little operation had a very good day. We should be celebrating. Like in televised sports. There should be specially made hats and shirts, people dousing each other with fizzy drinks . . . that sort of thing. We're definitely not shutting down."

"Technically horrible" is grounds for celebration, Kevin thought. *That's where expectations are set for me.*

119

They stopped at an intersection. They heard faint cheering from Wrigley Field, and a public address announcer's muffled voice.

"Cubs mighta scored," said Zach.

"Eh, not likely," said Kevin, "but you never know."

Cromwell licked Kevin's leg.

"Gross, Cromwell," he said.

Cromwell panted. Kevin sighed.

"Cromwell, it's possible that you and I are maybe just a little too fat, too prone to underachievement, and just too unlikely to succeed at real-world competitions."

"Oh, that's crazy," said Zach.

"*Overweight and Underachieving: My Life In and Out of Dog Shows.* By Kevin Leonard Pugh. Am I too young to write a memoir? Because I really think I have it in me to be a memoirist."

"Shut up," said Zach, shoving his friend.

Cromwell licked Kevin again.

"Gross. Seriously, Cromwell. I'm totally sweaty."

Another lick.

The walk continued in this way, Zach's enthusiasm beating against Kevin's pessimism, punctuated by licking.

In spite of their many excessively praised failures, Kevin faithfully trained with Cromwell leading up to the Paw Patch Invitational. They fell into a comfortable routine on off-days: sleep until late morning, then eat ... walk with Cromwell, then eat ... afternoon gaming ... agility training in the evening, then more gaming. And perhaps more eating.

Gradually the walks with Cromwell became longer walks at faster speeds. Then they became slouching jogs. Eventually they became full-out runs, with iPods and reflective shoes. At Elka's suggestion—and after training with her for a while, he obeyed all of her suggestions, which were actually polite commands—Kevin changed Cromwell's diet, asking his mom to buy a yellowish dog gruel. He couldn't actually pronounce the food's name—it had a few "ü's" and "ö's"—but it really seemed exotic, and appropriate for a dog in training.

"It's something like *Bloo-stoorppin-poofoogle*," Kevin told his mom. "Definitely starts with a 'B' and ends with an '-oogle.' I understand it's very good. For hips and joints."

"And I'm supposed to get it *where*?" his mom asked while writing *"B-oog-oogle"* on the dry-erase board. "I can't just go to PETCO? Or Dominick's? Or the Jewels?"

"Um ... an organic pet food shop somewhere in Wicker Park," Kevin said sheepishly. "On Damen, I think."

"Organic pet food," Maggie stated dryly.

"Yeah. And I think it's actually a 'boutique,' not a shop."

"Let's not tell anyone that part," said Howie.

"And why are we changing Cromwell's food again, Kevin?" asked Maggie, smiling.

"I . . . um . . . I was talking to this lady at the park. About, you know . . . dogs. And food. Her pugs like the, um . . . *Boog-stooplip-noogle*. Or whatever it's called."

"Okay, honey," said Kevin's mom.

To Kevin's surprise, Cromwell actually ate the new food—the first time it was served to him, and without hesitation.

Kevin still hadn't told his parents that he was training with Cromwell at Paw Patch, and they hadn't interrogated him about what he was doing with the time that was once devoted to camp, between the hours of 9:00 a.m. and noon on Mondays, Wednesdays, and Fridays. He realized that if he was out of sight, it was assumed that he was in the basement, on the couch. It was rare that anyone violated his domain. Izzy was about to qualify for some über-Olympic meta-intergalactic soccer thing—Kevin wasn't entirely sure about the details there—and everyone in the house seemed focused on it. He just knew that Cromwell was getting a little better at jumping and avoiding things—not imperceptibly better, but legitimately better. He was proud of his dog.

No one seemed to notice that Kevin was slowly weaning himself off the junkiest of the junk-food chips, too. When he left the house with Cromwell, he was sure that his family assumed he was going to Zach's. Even though he took no gaming gear, ever. And he never took the usual stash of cheese-flavored snacks.

On a Sunday night in mid-July, just days before the competition at Paw Patch, Maggie burst into the house with five shopping bags full of clothes.

"Kids!" she yelled. "Time for a back-to-school runway show!"

"Woo!" said Izzy from upstairs.

"Eww," said Kevin from the basement.

"Come on down here!" said Maggie, flinging her keys onto a table and plopping the bags on the carpet. "Or come up, as the case may be."

"It's way too early to think back-to-school, Mom," groaned Kevin.

"It's just two months away!" she replied.

Izzy and Kevin were each handed bags of clothes and dispatched to separate rooms to change, and to identify items that should be returned. The only thing rejected by Izzy was a grayish-blue sweater that "makes me look *exactly* like Aunt Connie! Eep!"

"Your aunt Connie is a lovely lady," said Maggie. "Isn't that right, Howie?"

Howie said nothing. His head was buried in a fantasy football draft guide. His eyes were narrowed, as if he were trying to read hieroglyphics by the light of a torch. Maggie ripped the magazine from his hands.

"Isn't Aunt Connie lovely, dear?"

"Yeah," he said. "I mean, she dresses like a fruitcup, but . . ."

Maggie threw the magazine into his lap.

"Fine," she said. "I'll take that one back. Kevin, how are you doing, hon?"

Kevin stepped into the living room looking as if he were wearing drapes. Or a parachute.

"These clothes are kinda big, Mom. I don't think I'm gonna grow into this, either. It's like a tent with sleeves."

"But, Kevin!" exclaimed Maggie. "I swear, that's just one size bigger than what you wore at the end of last school year!"

Everything she'd bought for him was, in fact, oversized. Kevin pulled the waistband of his jeans forward, revealing at least three inches of space where his midsection used to be. Maggie lifted his shirt slightly and tapped his belly, looking for ripples.

"Mom!" snapped Kevin, yanking the shirt down.

"Kevin," said Maggie, "I believe you've lost some weight." She turned toward Howie. "Howie . . ."

No response, so again she ripped the football magazine from his hands.

"Howie!" she said. "Look at your son."

"Cripes' sake, Kev," he said. "Where's the rest of you? When did you get so skinny?"

"Dad, I'm not exactly *skinny*," said Kevin, grabbing two inches of belly. "I've just had, um . . . an active summer."

His parents stared.

"It was all that football, maybe," added Kevin.

"He's gotten total exercise, Dad," confirmed Izzy. "He leaves with the dog, and they come back stinky sometimes."

"Hey!" said Kevin, though he wasn't particularly displeased.

His dad smiled.

"Well, it looks like you've got a parasite or somethin' in there. Maybe a . . . um, whatchamacallit . . . a heartworm."

"Pretty sure those are for dogs, Dad."

"Well, maybe you caught it from Cromwell," said Howie. "He's lookin' pretty trim these days, too."

The dog scampered up the basement steps at the mention of his name.

"So wait," said Kevin. "You noticed that the dog had lost some weight, but not *me*?"

"Well, he's made some dietary changes," said Howie. "I'm attentive. Don't think I'm not."

Riiiight, thought Kevin.

"Well, dear," said his mom, "I think I'll have to

125

take all those clothes back." Maggie stared at her old-
est child in clear disbelief. "Just when you think you
know someone . . ." She shook her head.

You really have no idea, Mom.

Kevin changed into workout attire and handed the
giant clothes back to his mother. He went outside to
stretch—he didn't want his family to see him in
agility-training mode. That would lead to questions,
and questions would lead to either lies or uncomfortable truths. Kevin withdrew a sophisticated digital
timer from his pocket, setting it to 0:00:00.000. Zach,
in his capacity as financier, had insisted on a timing
device for Cromwell that would be accurate to within
a thousandth of a second. Kevin had begun to use it
to time his treks to Paw Patch—he no longer took the
bike stroller—as well as neighborhood jogs.

"Okay, Cromwell," he said, then pressed a button
to start the clock.

It beeped once, and Kevin and Cromwell broke
into a run.

15

Kevin and Cromwell always ran the exact same path through Welles Park—this was essential, according to Zach, for accurate timing. They jogged past the same serious-looking lawn bowlers; past the tennis courts, where errant shots distracted Cromwell; past the soccer field, where adults played; and past a small, hunched-over ice cream man who persistently tempted Kevin with snow cones.

But Kevin averted his eyes and kept running.

Not fast, exactly. Other runners passed him, and he rarely passed anyone. He wiped sweat from his forehead with the back of his hand, then wiped the back of his hand on his T-shirt. Cromwell galloped, his tongue flopping. Kevin was singing along (badly, like an English-speaking sheep) to a random selection of songs on his iPod.

Park-goers stared. Some smiled. Others laughed. Kevin kept running.

He checked his timer.

0:10:36.007 . . .

The fractions of seconds ticked by, way too fast to follow. Kevin liked the meaningless precision. He checked again.

0:10:38.198 . . .

Kevin soon arrived at the south end of the park, emerging from the grass-lined path and onto an intersection at a side street that would lead east to North Clark. His head swiveled, checking for traffic, and then he urged Cromwell to cross.

But the dog had stopped.

Kevin looked down at Cromwell, who was barking—rather cheerfully—toward the street.

Looking up, Kevin saw his sister's grinning face poking out of the Bears-branded Tahoe. She waved. Kevin waved back. Then he saw his father chuckling behind the wheel, and his mom seated on the passenger side, a mixture of horror and amazement playing on her face.

Kevin shut off the iPod.

Seconds later, becoming acutely self-aware, he stopped singing. Cromwell kept woofing away.

"Oh, um . . . hey," said Kevin.

"Hey, yourself!" said his dad, somewhat mockingly. "Where are you in such a hurry to get to?"

"Nowhere," said Kevin. "Just running." He discreetly turned off the timer.

"You need to take it easy on this exercise, kid," said Howie. "It's critical to maintain your weight for football. We'll get you playin' again in the fall!"

Maggie slapped his arm.

"It's lovely that you're running, dear," she said. "We're all going to Water Tower right now so that I can return four hundred dollars' worth of clothes that won't fit you. And one nice—if somewhat old-fashioned—blue sweater. Would you like to join us?"

"C'mon!" Howie said. "Hop in, kid."

"No," said Kevin, breathing hard. "I'm good. Think I'll, um . . . head over to Zach's."

"That's, like, two miles away, Kev!" said his dad. "You're running away from Zach's right now."

"It's actually just 1.38 miles away," said Kevin. He immediately regretted the precision.

"Whoooooaa . . . ," said Howie. "Sor-*ry*, Mister GPS. My mistake." He laughed. "Well, would you like a 1.38-mile ride to Zachary's?" They stared at each other for a moment, father and son. Then Howie continued. "I'm telling you, Kev, big men like you and me—and there's still a big man in there, in spite of this clothes thing—we weren't necessarily built for jogging. We're not your long-distance types."

Kevin kept staring.

A car behind the Tahoe honked. Howie lifted his arms indignantly.

"Just havin' a conversation, here!" he shouted. Maggie waved the car around.

Cromwell whimpered. Kevin fingered the timer in his pocket.

"No, I don't need a ride," he said impatiently. "Or anything else . . . I'm good."

His family stared at him. Izzy chewed her gum.

"I tink it's gway you're jogging, Kev!" she said through the gum. "Looggin' good!"

Kevin stared at the ground, becoming even more self-conscious. "Thanks, Iz," he said.

Kevin wanted to take off, but his parents just . . . kept . . . *talking* . . .

"So have you really been jogging often, honey?" asked Maggie. She leaned across Howie to address her son.

"Well . . . ," Kevin said, "yeah. I mean . . . it's just jogging. You say it like you caught me shoplifting."

"Hey," said Howie, pointing a finger at his son. "You know I had my first encounter with the police when I was jus—"

Maggie swatted her husband's arm again, this time with somewhat more force.

"Wrong lesson, dear," she said tersely. Then she turned back to Kevin.

"No one's saying it's a bad thing, this jogging. It's just not ... um ..." Maggie looked away. "It's not really typical of you."

"How the heck would you even *know* what's 'typical' of me?" asked Kevin.

Cromwell whined again, then bumped Kevin's leg with his nose.

"Does anyone know what a typical day is for me?" demanded Kevin. His annoyance was rising. "Anyone? Any guesses?"

Howie pulled the Tahoe to the curb.

"Listen, Kev," he began, "I mean ... I think we got your schedule pretty well down: sleep, eat, TV, eat, TV, slee—"

"See, that's just what I mean!" Kevin huffed.

But he recognized that he was going too far. He wasn't prepared to disclose the training with Elka; not now. That might involve a discussion of the unspoken arrangement with Coach Z. And that was a conversation he didn't want to have, ever. It was actually convenient to have everyone think that he was the same old Kevin Pugh, with couch potato tendencies but a newfound interest in fitness.

"What *do* you mean, Kev?" asked his dad.

"I just ... well, okay, it's true that there is some eating and some TV. But you think that's, like, my whole life?"

Before Howie could nod in response, Maggie delivered another small swat.

"Well, it's not," continued Kevin. "I just don't want you to think I'm completely inert. I move. I train."

"For football, yeah?" asked Howie.

Not in a thousand lifetimes, no, thought Kevin.

"Well, sure," he said. He stared at his father, unblinking.

"He is eating all weird," said Izzy, removing her gum. "That's for sure."

"The boy was born eatin' weird," said Howie. "Had his first McRib before he even had baby teeth."

"No," said Izzy, "I mean, like, he's been eating good stuff—non–fast food stuff. And fewer snack cakes, too."

"Is that right, Kev?" asked Howie. "Really?" It was almost as if his son were being accused of witchcraft.

"Yes, Dad." Kevin shook his head and groaned. "Come on, Cromwell."

Kevin tugged at the dog's leash, and the pair took a few quick steps.

Howie lurched the SUV forward and leaned his head out the window.

"Hey!" he yelled. "We're tryin' to talk to you, Kev. Come on . . . you say we don't ask things, so here we are, asking."

Kevin stopped.

"Yes, Dad, I have been eating a little differently."

"For football?" asked Howie.

Heck no, thought Kevin.

"Right," he said. Kevin then looked at Maggie. "You actually buy the food, Mom. You haven't noticed that I'm not eating just chips and cream-filled snack cakes? At all? You really haven't noticed?"

She opened her mouth, but said nothing.

"I eat bananas and apples and stuff lately—right in front of you! Like at the table, in full view of everyone. Izzy can confirm it."

"I think your, um . . . your weight loss initiative is lovely, Kevin," said Maggie tentatively.

"It's not a *weight loss* initiative!" Kevin said.

"It's a football initiative," said Howie, evidently satisfied. He honked the horn, which, of course, played the chorus of "The Super Bowl Shuffle."

"Ohmy*gawd,* ohmygawd!" said an excited passerby. He wore a backwards Bears cap and his mouth was hanging open. "You're Howie Pugh! Oh . . . my . . . *God . . .*"

"Hey, how ya doin', kid," said Howie with a practiced grin.

He wasn't actually speaking to a kid, of course, but to a large grown adult male. But to Kevin, the dude looked a bit childish, fawning in front of his dad like that.

The man looked back and forth between Kevin and Howie.

"I . . . I'm totally sorry," he stammered. "I'm interrupting. Very sorry." Flustered, he dug into a pocket, withdrew a pen, and removed his cap. "If I could just maybe get you to sign the cap, Mr. Pugh, that'd be *so* awesome . . . I'm a *huge* fan. . . ."

"Sure thing, kid." Howie took the pen and the cap.

"Saw you play, back in the day," continued the fan. "You were awesome. . . ."

"Thanks, kid."

Kevin turned on his iPod, clicked the timer, and tugged at Cromwell's leash. He caught Izzy's eye, then quickly spun on his heels and ran. Kevin furrowed his brow and dropped his head. The dog bounced happily beside him.

"You could sign hats someday," he grumbled to Cromwell. The dog woofed. "Or dog sweaters, or something."

Kevin arrived at Zach's house drained from the jog, demanding virtual competition. Zach, of course, obliged.

Down arrow . . . left arrow . . . "A" button . . .

"You're getting better in coverage," Kevin said.

"Hmpf," said Zach. "I don't need your pity."

"No, you tackled me almost right after the catch there—that 37-yard catch."

"A" button . . . left arrow . . . right arrow . . .

"So are you sure that was the best move, not just telling your mom and dad about the agility stuff?" said Zach.

"No," answered Kevin. "I don't know the best move, exactly. I don't wanna talk about it. I'd rather talk about how you can't stop the Waggle."

Up arrow . . . up arrow . . . left arrow . . . "A" button . . .

"You'll eventually need to have the dog-versus-football talk."

"But not *now*. With *you*."

"Well, no, but . . ."

". . . but you want to make sure your investment is secure."

Zach was silent for a moment, then said, "Maybe."

"Well, it's secure. I'm just putting off the talk. Maybe until after the thing this week."

"The Paw Patch Invitational?"

"That's the one."

"A" button . . . "A" button . . . "B" button . . .

"Elka says that the top finisher moves on to some Midwest Kennel something-something championships. This is apparently a big deal—it's at the United Center." Kevin's thumb pounded the controller. "This is what she says."

"Dude! Team Cromwell will *dominate*. Your dog is a

bolt of furry lightning! He's a, a, a . . . well, he's going to dominate!"

"Two things wrong with that," said Kevin. "One, *I* am not a bolt of lightning. And two, Cromwell is not at all times what you would call disciplined. He moves fast—weirdly fast. But the deductions add up. That's what kills us. We always have, like, two minutes of penalties."

"As the manager of Team Cromwell, these are shortcomings that I expect you—my employee—to address."

"Workin' on it, boss," said Kevin.

Up arrow . . . left arrow . . . up arrow . . .

Kevin intercepted Zach's quarterback's pass.

"Sweet!" said Kevin.

"Gaaaaaarrgh," said Zach.

"Touchdown!" said Kevin.

"We need to make T-shirts."

"Dude, I beat you at Madden all the time. It's not really a shirt-worthy achievement."

"No, fool. For Team Cromwell—we need T-shirts. For the Paw Patch thing. And then we'll need 'em for the Midwest Kennel blah-bitty-blah championships."

"Which, just to be clear, we won't qualify for."

"Whatever, Kevin. We need uniforms."

Kevin snickered.

"We'll get jerseys. Howie Pugh respects sports with jerseys, right?" asked Zach.

"I can't imagine Howie appreciating anything about his son and dog jumping over little plastic obstacles, actually."

"Who's the best dog at Paw Patch?" asked Zach.

"Why, are you gonna do something to them? Like send threats, written in dog language? Or poison their kibble?"

"I like your cutthroat attitude, Kevin. But no. Just scouting the competition. If you're going to be the best, you have to beat the best. That's what they say in sports. At least that's what they say on SportsCenter."

"There's no *best* dog, really," said Kevin. "Elka has trained an army of drones. You've seen 'em. They're like machines, little dog-bots." A virtual broadcaster was excitedly discussing the details of an on-screen injury. "I think most of the reason Elka likes Cromwell is that she hasn't exactly made him a dog-bot quite yet."

"He's like a dog stallion," said Zach. "Can't break him. Run free, li'l furry stallion."

"You're odd," said Kevin.

"B" button . . . up arrow . . . left arrow . . .

"And you need to choose your receivers a little quicker."

Up arrow . . . left arrow . . . up arrow . . .

"Another touchdown," Kevin said flatly.

"Try to keep some of this dominance in reserve for the invitational, dude."

Kevin smiled. "Sorry, buddy. It's hard to control. You just never know when the awesomeness will burst forth."

16

Kevin and Cromwell continued their daily training runs up to that Friday, the day of the Invitational, and their times continued to improve, if only slightly. Izzy ran with them once and—to Kevin's total astonishment—she actually seemed tired when it was over. The Monday and Wednesday sessions with Elka went reasonably well, too, but Cromwell remained a deduction machine. He collided with too many things to ever post a seriously competitive time. Cromwell didn't actually break any obstacles or dogs, though, and that seemed like a promising development.

Despite the fact that they'd jogged together, Kevin had still said nothing to his sister about dog agility—or to anyone else. It had become a weight he carried with him. Would his parents actually mind? Probably.

His dad certainly would. These were the classes that he refused to pay for, after all. Would this raise more questions about Kevin's future commitment to football? Or worse, about his departure from camp at Scherzer? Possibly. The risks of discussing dog agility were too many, Kevin decided, and the benefits were too few.

He might have been nervous on Friday morning, were it not for his certainty about the results—they were going to finish near the bottom of the field, no question. Expectations were low all around. So no need to worry.

Zach, however, seemed unusually edgy.

"Big day for us," he whispered to Kevin as the friends and family of Paw Patch clients filtered into the training area. "*Huge* day." Zach cracked his knuckles, a nervous habit. "Just huge."

"Sweet shirt," said Kevin, mockingly.

Zach tugged at the bottom of his mesh jersey, then admired the green lettering:

TEAM
CROMWELL

Below the name was a very large number 1.

"I think it's sweet," said Zach, still whispering. "You should wear yours, dude. In fact, you should do whatever I ask. Let's try to remember who's funding this operation."

"Even if you gave me every cent of your three-thousand-and-whatever dollars you've got left, I still wouldn't wear that jersey," said Kevin. "No way, no chance. It's teal. Not a good color for me."

Cromwell began bouncing excitedly as dogs and their handlers lined up along the sidelines of the course.

Elka had arranged a refreshments table with an awful-looking reddish-brown punch, onion crackers, unpleasant-looking cheese, and some sort of uniden-tifiable fruit that wasn't quite orange but not exactly pink. There were also dog treats and rawhides.

Cromwell continued to bounce, and soon began to whine.

"Shhh," said Kevin. "It's okay, boy." He stroked the dog's head.

"Maybe he wants his jersey," said Zach. "It might calm him down." He produced a smaller teal shirt from his backpack.

"No, um . . . I think the jersey would freak him out more. He's not a clothes-wearing kind of dog."

"But it's chilly in here," said Zach. "He might . . ."

Elka interrupted the conversation, sweeping in front of Zach to greet Kevin with unusual warmth. She put an arm across his shoulder and grinned wide.

"So nice to see you, Mr. Pugh."

"Um, I'm here, you know . . . pretty much three days a week."

"Ah, but this is a *special* day, I think. Are your parents here?"

"They, um . . . no, they have, um . . ."

"Very sorry," said Elka. "I should like to meet the parents of such a marvelous dog, and his occasionally determined handler." She winked, which she'd never done before, at least in Kevin's presence. "The manager is here, I see," she said, smirking at Zach. "Have you boys tried the fruit? The cheese? So delicious. They are my favorites."

Cromwell whined again, this time in a way that couldn't be mistaken for anything but anxiousness. Elka dropped to the ground, held his face in her hands for a moment, and then lifted his ear and whispered something. Cromwell made the half-laughing noise that only Elka could induce. He then ceased whining. He didn't quite stop bouncing, though.

Elka stood up quickly and examined Zach's jersey.

"We are not some silly *sport*, Zachary," she said, as if a sport was the lowest thing anything could be.

"Hey." Zach grinned. "That's what Kevin's dad says, too!"

"Well, he is a very shrewd man," said Elka,

marching off to her platform. Cromwell grew quiet and attentive.

"Not especially," muttered Kevin.

Elka stepped onto her perch.

"Welcome, students of Paw Patch!" she announced over the buzzing. At the sound of her voice, the room grew quiet. "Today is a *very* special day for me!"

"You know it's special," Zach whispered in a voice that was barely audible, "because she wore a paisley headscarf."

Elka gave him a suspicious stare as she continued.

"We have assembled this morning for the twentieth annual Paw Patch Invitational! I must say, I'm so pleased to see the faces of so many alums here today." She gave a small wave toward a group of visitors that Kevin didn't recognize.

"Dude, I'm not coming back for the fortieth," whispered Zach. "Just so you know."

Elka shot a wicked glare in his direction. Zach gulped.

"Paw Patch is a labor of love for me," said Elka to the group. "It is my great pleasure to have worked with all of you—and with your lovely dogs."

Applause filled the room. Zach clapped enthusiastically, as if to make up for his earlier transgressions.

Kevin tried to estimate the number of attendees at the invitational, but there were too many for him to count. He'd never seen the training area packed so tightly. He felt the first flutter of worry.

"Before we begin today's exhibition, I would like to introduce two extraordinary guests who have been kind enough to join us." Elka beamed, which was rare for her. "They are well-known in the agility community, and I'm *so* excited to have them here all the way from Schaumburg . . ." Elka twirled around, facing a door at the rear of the room. "Please extend a glorious welcome to Jody and Shasta Gatkowski!"

The room was soon filled with oohs and shrieks and other exclamations of delight. Applause built as the small black-haired girl and her small black-haired dog entered the training room. The girl's hair was pulled back tight. She wore a red polo with various pet industry logos; black shorts; and red athletic shoes. They were followed by a very large man— apparently a bodyguard—wearing a Bluetooth earpiece. He scanned the room with cold eyes. The girl gave a practiced wave and a bright (yet clearly fake) smile.

"Who is *she?*" asked Zach. He was no longer whispering, since the training room was as noisy as it had ever been.

"She's kinda famous, at least in the dog world," said Kevin. "She wins things. In fact, she might win everything." Cameras flashed. Kevin nudged Zach and pointed to the terrier. "*That* is the dog that made Cromwell go crazy for this stuff in the first place— that's the TV dog, the Animal Planet dog."

"Then *that*," said Zach, "is our competition."

"Right," said Kevin. "In the same way that Orlando Bloom is my dating competition."

"Don't sell yourself short, dude," said Zach.

"Those two are maybe a little out of our league," Kevin said quietly.

Jody, Shasta, and the towering Bluetooth goon approached Elka. The girl grinned, the dog wagged, and the goon looked angry.

"They bring their own security?" asked Zach.

"I told you," said Kevin. "They're a big deal."

The applause had not subsided. Elka clasped her hands and smiled as if she'd never been more pleased. She embraced the girl, although Kevin thought it was an insincere, minimal-contact sort of hug.

"Students!" called Elka, quieting the crowd. "Whoever among you qualifies for the Midwest Kennel Club Championship will have the privilege of competing alongside Jody and Shasta."

"Won't be us," whispered Kevin.

"*Might* be," answered Zach, not in a whisper.

This drew another quick look from Elka. She cleared her throat, then spoke again.

"Of course these two great champions do not need to qualify, because . . . well, how many MKCC titles have you won, dear?"

"Four straight!" answered the girl, grinning.

"They are *quite* accomplished," said Elka. "We're fortunate they've agreed to share some time with us today."

Cromwell fidgeted at Kevin's feet.

Elka clapped her hands and said, "Perhaps Jody and Shasta would be willing to give us a small demonstration?"

This elicited more cheering from the audience—excluding Zach—and howling from a few of the dogs.

"Of course, Ms. Brandt," said the girl in a nasal voice. She had an impossibly broad smile, like an excited pageant contestant. "I'd *love* to help your students!"

The girl turned, snapped a finger, and pointed. The terrier moved to the starting line of the agility course with unthinkable speed—almost as if by teleportation. The girl then rushed to the dog's side. She whistled, then made eye contact with her terrier, then said, *"Go, girl!"*

And the girls went.

Kevin had never seen creatures move quite like them. They were a blur of limbs, never slowing, cutting precisely—it was an amazing performance, really. They made almost no sound at all, not even when the dog fired herself through the hoop at the course's end.

"Whoa," said Zach.

"Yeah," said Kevin. "If anybody here should have jerseys and sponsors . . ."

"Okay, it's probably them. But you're a close second, Kev."

"Actually, I think I'm a distant seventeenth." He looked down at his dog. "But who's counting?"

Cromwell woofed.

Jody and Shasta eased to a stop beside Elka, and the audience roared in approval—including Zach. The girl took several exaggerated bows. Her terrier sat perfectly still, as if she were experiencing total adulation for the millionth time. Which, Kevin thought, she probably was.

The security goon folded his arms. Elka clapped. The girl blew kisses.

"My friends," said Elka, "*that* is what you're working toward. Brilliant!"

More bowing, more air-smooching, more applauding.

Cromwell fussed a little more, lifting his head toward Kevin, then pawing the AstroTurf.

"Looks like our boy is fired up!" said Zach.

Cromwell pawed Kevin's leg, then barked.

"Or he's freaked," said Kevin. "Either way, we really need to get this thing over with."

17

Much to Kevin's disappointment, he and Cromwell did not go first—that honor was for Willamina.

They did not go second, either—that was Tinkles.

Or ninth—that was Vladimir.

Or twelfth—that was a Newfoundland named Constantine Tazmanius III. (And yes, there had been a Tazmanius I and II.)

Kevin and Cromwell waited . . . and waited . . . and waited. They watched each dog-and-handler combination go before them—everyone in the class. Friends and family clapped in approval. Kevin was fairly sure that Elka eyed Cromwell after each of the runs, and that they shared a look of some sort. He wondered if he should feel jealous, having another person connect with his dog in some psychic, wordless way. But that seemed selfish. Cromwell should be allowed other friends, Kevin concluded.

The dog rubbed against the AstroTurf, then woofed. Then he jumped.

"Stay loose, boy," said Zach.

Hard to say if he's loose or tight, thought Kevin. *But he's definitely something.*

Jody and Shasta and their goon hadn't left. They stood patiently along a far wall, signing autographs, posing for photos, glancing toward the course every so often.

Kevin's classmates all put up similar times, regardless of the age and shape of the handler or the age, shape, and breed of the dog. The leader was a golden retriever named Melvin, with a time of 55.9 seconds. Trailing him were a shepherd-chow mix named Bodie at 56.2 and, to Kevin's surprise, the resilient shih-poo, Tinkles, at 56.7.

Scoring and timing were handled by Elka, and she betrayed no emotion while monitoring the course. It was the usual series of obstacles: running up ramps, down ramps, over hurdles, and through three different tubes; weaving through a series of poles; coming to a full stop on a small table; leaping the little windmill; scrambling over the seesaw; and jumping through a hoop. It was a route that Cromwell had run (improperly, though not slowly) dozens of times. The hoop in particular gave Cromwell fits. It was slightly higher than the tire swing in the Pughs' backyard—the one Cromwell had never quite mastered. Often he just bashed his head into the bottom of the hoop and streaked on. Kevin wasn't particularly good at convincing Cromwell to repeat the obstacles he missed, and this led to enormous, unconquerable time penalties.

The dog continued his jumping.

"Chill, Crom," said Kevin. "At this point, there's really no need to hurry up and lose."

All the other dogs and handlers were either mingling with each other or fawning over Jody and Shasta. Many were already congratulating Melvin and his owner, a stout woman named Mandy.

Kevin and Cromwell simply waited. They had not yet been called.

"Check this out, dude," said Zach. He motioned toward the goon, who was clearing a path for Jody and Shasta to leave.

"Please, everyone, please," said Elka, just loud enough to hush most of the conversations. "Let's give our final competitors your attention. Allow me to introduce Cromwell, a precocious beagle mix, and his owner, Mr. Kevin Pugh."

Zach clapped energetically. He was leaning against the wall, wearing sunglasses and the Team Cromwell jersey. Some others clapped politely. Then Zach whistled, alarming a few dogs. And then he woofed, which brought responses from *many* dogs.

"Thank you, Zachary," said Elka, flashing him a stern look. "Your contributions have not gone unnoticed today."

Cromwell made a low *rrrrrroooo*-ing sort of sound.

Kevin felt a surge of nervous energy as he walked his dog to the starting line. He caught a glimpse of Jody and Shasta from the corner of his eye. They were exiting slowly, moving toward the door from which they'd made their triumphant entrance.

Maybe I should stall until they're gone, thought Kevin.

"Whenever you're ready . . . ," said Elka.

Kevin contemplated his readiness. Cromwell shook off a bit of slobber.

Elka took a step toward them and spoke softly.

"Remember, we compete only against the course, Mr. Pugh. Nothing else."

Kevin nodded, but he was still looking at the crowd.

"Nothing else," repeated Elka.

Kevin glanced at the course, then toward his dog. His eyes began to trace the path between obstacles. The crowd noise faded and the world seemed to slow. Kevin looked back at Elka. Her mouth was moving, but he couldn't quite hear her. He assumed she was telling him to start whenever he and the dog were ready.

When he saw Cromwell staring up at him, Kevin knew it was time.

"Go," he said firmly.

Cromwell did.

He flew off the starting line, a blur of spinning paws and flopping ears. Kevin kept Cromwell's pace—barely—darting ahead of him through the course, spitting out directions and encouragement.

Cromwell raced up the A-frame ramp, then down the other side . . .

He leapt three hurdles, each with room to spare . . .

He scurried through the fabric cylinder that Elka called a "collapsed tunnel" . . .

He jumped more hurdles, his tail just nicking one . . .

He clambered up an incline, across a plank, then back down . . .

He looped through a U-shaped vinyl tunnel . . .

He hopped onto the table, where he was supposed to pause—and to Kevin's amazement, he actually froze for an instant, like a statue . . .

And then he was off again, streaking through the weave poles easily . . .

Then onto the edge of the seesaw, climbing cautiously . . . up . . . and up . . . pausing . . . and then racing down the seesaw, from which he always, *always,* *ALWAYS* had seemed to jump too early—but not this time! All four paws crossed over to the contact point, and Cromwell leapt off, totally in control . . .

He eyed the hoop—the final obstacle—and ran for it, paws churning. Kevin raced with him, hoping he could get his dog to wait for *just* the proper instant to jump, as there was no margin for error with Cromwell and hoops . . .

"Wait," said Kevin. "Wait . . . Wait . . ."

Cromwell neared the mark, perhaps three feet from the hoop . . .

"Now!" shouted Kevin.

Cromwell leapt, poking his face through, stretching . . .

. . . and his front paws made it, followed narrowly by his belly!

He scraped the hoop with his fur, his tail, and his rear paws. The hoop wobbled, but Cromwell hit the ground only slightly askew and raced to the finish.

"Yeah!" exclaimed Kevin, skidding to a stop near Elka's platform.

Suddenly he noticed the crowd again.

Zach was hooting, and Elka evidently wasn't stopping him. The audience applauded—and not tepidly, as before, but with real enthusiasm. A low murmur rolled through the room like a wave.

Cromwell panted and ran in a tight circle. Kevin crouched down to pet him, but Cromwell leapt into his arms, scampered atop his shoulders, and then hopped off—almost gracefully.

Kevin's eyes sought out the official clock. It was blinking near the starting line: 0:00:49.600.

"No . . . way . . . ," he said quietly.

It had been, by at least fifteen seconds, the fastest run of Cromwell's life. Kevin also felt quite sure that it was the least flawed run of Cromwell's life. He stared at the clock for a few seconds in disbelief.

Then Zach leapt onto Kevin's back, still hooting, and two-thirds of Team Cromwell tumbled to the ground. There they encountered the other third of Team Cromwell, who started licking them.

Elka made notes on a scorecard, then smiled at Cromwell.

"Not bad, Mr. Pugh," she said. "A fine effort. A bit rough on the hoop, but not so bad at all."

Kevin stood there, grinning.

"That was our best run ever!" he declared. "By a mile!"

"There is no doubting that," said Elka. "But the hoop was a bit rough."

"No," laughed Kevin. "What just happened out there was a miracle! 'A bit rough' is when you have to remove your fat dog from his backyard swing twenty times a night because he can't jump through it and won't stop trying."

"Mr. Pugh," said Elka firmly, "you are no longer in your backyard. We have not yet seen the best of this beautiful dog—and it's your job to find it."

"Uhhh . . . okay, yeah," Kevin said.

Can't see how the beautiful dog is going to top this, he thought. *But okay.*

Kevin smiled and stared at the clock as it blinked his time.

"You will need to find Cromwell's very best for the North American Dog Agility Council Championship, that much is certain."

Zach shoved Kevin gleefully. Being somewhat larger than Zach, Kevin didn't actually move when Zach shoved him. Instead, Zach tipped back and landed with a thud on the AstroTurf.

Elka grinned. Classmates swirled around, offering congratulations.

"S-so . . . I'm going to the United Center?" stammered Kevin. "But weren't there penal—?"

"Mr. Pugh!" said Elka. "Cromwell was six seconds faster than every other dog in the room!"

"Well," said a nasal voice, "not faster than *every* dog."

Kevin turned slowly. Directly in front of him stood the security goon. And directly behind the goon, peeking around his bulk, were Jody and Shasta.

"Hey, whassup?" said Zach, not coolly.

The girl ignored him. Instead, she smirked at Cromwell and Kevin.

"She seems a little angry, dude," whispered Zach.

The terrier seemed content enough. It sniffed at Cromwell and he sniffed back.

But the girl sneered. She eyed Kevin the way policemen eye suspects in TV crime dramas. She was at least a full head shorter than him, he noticed. She was also somewhat older, and rail-thin. She said nothing. Just kept sneering.

"Uh . . . hello," Kevin finally said. "I'm, uh . . ."

"Kevin Poo," she said. "That's your name, isn't it?"

The terrier sat panting, along with Cromwell.

"It's um . . . well, no," said Kevin. "It's Pugh. It's pronounced Pee-*yoo*."

She simply stared.

"You guys were amazing," Kevin offered. "Truly amazing. I've never seen anything quite li—"

"I know," snapped the girl.

"Yeah, absolutely. I saw you guys win the, um . . . well, I don't know what the competition was called, but it was on televi—"

"The Purina Incredible Dog Challenge," she said. "It's just the single most important event on the agility calendar, that's all." She paused. "And we won it. But that's okay if you can't think of the name."

"No, well, I don't mean to disrespect anyone," said

157

Kevin. "Or anything. Certainly not a delicious dog food. Not that I know *personally* that it's delicious, but Cromwell used to . . ."

"Whatever, Poo," said the girl. She tapped the goon on the back. "C'mon, Dad, we've gotta roll."

"Oh, that's your *dad*," said Kevin. "Because we were thinking he was some sort of bodyguard or enforce—"

The Bluetooth goon stared at Kevin angrily.

"Um . . . yeah," said Kevin. "Well, it was very nice to meet your lovely family."

"I'm sure it was, Poo," said the girl. She spun around and marched toward the exit, the terrier at her side in perfect sync. "See you in two weeks," she called.

Kevin looked at Elka.

"Two weeks?" he asked.

"Yes, well, the MKCC is rather soon," Elka said. "I had not imagined that Cromwell could be ready for an event of this magnitude until perhaps next summer. Maybe March or April at the earliest." She shook her head in apparent disbelief. "And actually, Mr. Pugh, I was not sure you'd commit to your training for so long. Not through the school year."

Kevin didn't immediately dispute this, though Zach did.

"Team Cromwell is the future of dog agility! Yeah, baby!"

"Zachary, I can only assume that you were not referring to me as 'baby' just then."

"No!" he said. "I meant the collective 'baby.' Not one 'baby' in particular."

"Well," said Elka, "if you feel that you are indeed the future of agility championships—and I assure you, there are many possible futures—then you should know that the future arrives in thirteen days."

18

That afternoon, the Pughs' front door swung open with a loud crack and Cromwell burst inside, barking. Howie rolled off the living room sofa.

"Yeesh!" he said, clearly startled.

Howie was crouching defensively—a pose not unlike the one on his 1981 football card.

"What the . . . Cromwell? Whatcha . . ."

The dog charged, launching both paws into Howie's chest and toppling him over. Then Cromwell stood on Howie's rounded midsection, licked his face several times, and hopped off, racing down a hallway.

Kevin and Zach stood in the entryway, laughing.

"I'm glad you're amused by the fact that I've just been assaulted by the family dog," said Kevin's dad.

"He's not a dog," said Zach. "He's a high-performance machine."

Kevin gave his friend a playful shove. This was followed by more laughter.

Somewhere in the distance there was a faint shriek from Maggie, followed by more barking from Cromwell.

"What the heck did you do to the dog, Kev?" asked Howie. "He's a little wound up today. I kinda miss the old Cromwell, with the sleeping and the eating . . . and none of this jumpy stuff. Not sure I can get used to this dog."

"I'm serious, Mr. Pugh!" yelped Zach. "He's not a dog, he's a machi—!"

"A machine," said Howie. "Right. Got it." He settled himself back on the couch, tossing his *Sun-Times* onto the coffee table. Howie stared at Kevin, though not with disapproval.

"He's just in a good mood," said Kevin, smiling. "He's an active dog."

Cromwell thundered back down the stairs, zoomed past the couch again, and then rolled to a stop at Kevin's feet.

Zach hooted loudly.

"Please don't *whoo* in my house," said Howie.

"Sorry, sir," said Zach, as calmly as he could.

Kevin grabbed his friend by the arm and motioned to the basement.

"You'll be in your office, Kev?" asked Howie smugly. He readjusted himself on the sofa.

"Sure will, Dad."

As soon as Kevin, Zach, and Cromwell reached the bottom of the stairs, Zach removed the Team Cromwell jersey from his backpack and pulled it over his head.

"I can't believe you made me take this off, dude!"

"Might've been tough to explain it to my parents. You know, if they happened to ask what 'Team Cromwell' was, and why you were on it."

Zach dug a little deeper in the backpack and extracted a bone-shaped trophy. Engraved on the bottom were these words: "CHAMPION—PAW PATCH INV'L."

Zach tapped the lettering with his index finger.

"You see that? It says 'Champion.' That's us. And we're not finished . . . oh, no. This was merely our first—and certainly not our last—piece of hardware. I really couldn't have done it without you, Kevin, because . . ."

"Because I own the dog. And I do all the running."

"Right," said Zach. "Anyway, you should take this trophy, put on your jersey—which you *still* haven't worn—and march back upstairs. Slam this little beauty down on the coffee table and tell your dad that not only are you and Cromwell enrolled in agility classes, but you're *dominating*!"

Cromwell pounced on the basement couch, sniffed the pillows, and then licked himself.

"Zach," said Kevin, "we've never dominated."

"Until today."

"Right," said Kevin, walking over to his dog. "And it was great. But it was also kind of a fluke. Cromwell has only made it through that stinkin' hoop *once* . . ."

"And that one time was *today,* with the pressure on. When it mattered most." Zach joined the rest of Team Cromwell on the couch. "Your dog is clutch, dude. You can't deny it."

"No," Kevin said, looking down at Cromwell. "I can't deny it. He does seem to be clutchy. You sure were today, boy." Kevin scratched Cromwell behind his ears. The dog craned his neck, then licked Kevin's chin.

"So what you've gotta do," said Zach, "is take the trophy, put on the jersey, and march back up—"

Kevin heard the creak of his father's feet on the basement steps. He snatched the trophy, tossed it to Zach, and then smothered the hardware and the Team Cromwell jersey with a large animal-print pillow.

"Not a word!" he commanded in a whisper. "And don't move the pillow!"

"Hey!" said Zach. "You can't boss me around! I'm the mana—"

"Boys," began Howie, now standing at the bottom

of the stairs. "I've gotta go. There's a collectibles show out in Rosemont. I'm autographing this afternoon."

"Signing little helmets for little men," said Kevin.

"That's what your mother calls it," said Howie. "Good money in those li'l men."

"I'm sure there is," said Kevin.

"Good money in little dogs, too," said Zach, grinning.

Howie looked at him quizzically. Kevin looked at him angrily.

"O-*kaaaay*," said Howie. "But to the best of my knowledge, no dog has ever spent thirty-five bucks to wait in my autograph line."

Kevin elbowed the pillow that covered the evidence of Cromwell's agility triumph. The dog himself had fallen asleep.

"So we'll see you later, Dad," said Kevin. "Buh-bye."

"Kev," said Howie, "I was thinking that maybe when I get back tonight we could throw the ball around."

"Um . . . sure," said Kevin. "Which ball?"

"The *football*, kid!" Howie smiled, then placed a foot on the stairs and jingled his car keys. "Your mom and I were . . . well, we're impressed by the training, Kev. The jogging and whatnot. I don't think we made that clear the other day."

Not perfectly, thought Kevin.

The father stared at his son. The son fidgeted.

"Yeah, um . . . thanks, Dad. Cool." He paused. "Bye."

"Okay," said Howie. "Later, boys." He clomped back up the steps.

Kevin waited patiently for the sound of the kitchen door opening and closing, then ripped the pillow away from Zach and began pummeling him.

THWAP!

"Oooof!" shouted his friend, laughing.

Cromwell stirred. Kevin delivered a series of pillow shots to Zach's gut.

THWAP! THWAP! THWAP!

Cromwell woke up, slid off the couch, and curled into a ball on the floor.

THWAP! THWAP! THWAP!

"Hey!" exclaimed Zach. "Stop! No more!"

Kevin paused, lowering the pillow, breathing hard. Zach was shielding his face with his forearms, but still giggling.

"It's not funny!" said Kevin. "You are *not* authorized to speak to my parents unless spoken to!"

"Okay, okay . . . ," said Zach. "But we can't keep Team Cromwell a secret for long." Zach lowered his arms. "We're gonna be huge, Kev. *Huge,* I tell you—"

THWAP!

Zach took a pillow to the face and fell from the couch.

"Okay," he muttered. "That was a cheap shot." He sat on the floor with his back against the couch.

Both Zach and Kevin stared down at the dog, who was napping again. Cromwell had managed to find the one sliver of sunlight that cut across an otherwise dark basement. Kevin held the trophy aloft, examining it as if it were an ancient artifact.

"You could get used to winning those, right?" asked Zach.

Kevin was quiet for a moment.

"Sure," he finally said. "I guess so."

Zach pressed on.

"We need to discuss what the business world calls 'next steps,' Kevin."

"We need to *what*?"

"I'm just saying that we need to evaluate ways to take advantage of the major step—and I mean *major* step—that Team Cromwell took today."

"What are you talking about, dude?" asked Kevin.

"I'm talking about merchandising," said Zach. "I'm talking about marketing. I'm talking about a dog with charisma that never quits."

Cromwell made a loud snuffling sound in his sleep.

"See," said Zach. "Even when he sleeps, he's got presence. He has a certain air."

"He farts in his sleep. Always has."

"We'll hide that fact from the press." Zach snorted. Then he stood up. "Cromwell is going to revolutionize the sport of dog agility, dude."

"It's not a sport," said Kevin wryly. "My dad said so, remember? And he's a sports professional. An insider. He knows these things."

"Well, whatever it is, Cromwell is taking it over."

"Dude," said Kevin, rolling his eyes. "We beat sixteen dogs today. That's it. And it took the best run of Cromwell's life."

"But those were sixteen of the . . ."

"Of the *what*?" asked Kevin. "Of the most agile dogs on the North Side of Chicago?" Kevin stretched himself out on the sofa. "Maybe Cromwell and I should retire now, covered in glory. We're winners— maybe not at the highest level, but at least at some level. Why keep going? Are we supposed to just keep doing this until we qualify for an event where we can finish last? Just keep going till you lose—is that the point?"

"You don't mean that," said Zach. "You know you like it."

Kevin smiled, then examined the trophy again. Zach pressed on.

"You won't stop and you know it—not unless you're able to pay back your investor. Can you do that?"

Kevin laughed.

"Admit that you sort of want to see what the non-Elka world of dog agility looks like," said Zach. "Come on . . ."

"Okay, I do," said Kevin. "But if it looks anything like Jody and Shasta, then it's out of our league."

"Elka seemed happy for Cromwell tonight," said Zach. "Perhaps a little miffed with me, for whatever reason."

"Anytime Cromwell doesn't destroy her equipment, it's a success," said Kevin.

"Hey, don't sell the dog short," said Zach.

"He's not a dog, he's a . . ."

". . . a high-performance machine. So true."

The machine farted, then rolled over.

19

Although Kevin was not generally prone to bouts of confidence, he felt unusually accomplished in the days following the Paw Patch Invitational. He carried himself differently, his chin raised a little higher, his voice just slightly louder. He doodled *"0:00:49.600"* everywhere. When Kevin jogged with Cromwell, he made eye contact with other joggers—this was an entirely new habit. Sometimes he even smiled at them. Occasionally he passed someone.

He couldn't actually keep the trophy in plain view, of course, so he hid it under his mattress at the foot of his bed. He retrieved it from time to time, inspecting it, reminding himself of his new place in the dog agility hierarchy. In particular, he enjoyed the memory of his conversation with the reigning champion of the Purina Challenge (and of every other meaning-ful agility event). She seemed legitimately miffed—possibly even rattled—by Kevin and Cromwell's run. That thought brought him great satisfaction, since he had decided that the girl was fundamentally evil.

All things considered, life was going well for Kevin Pugh, just shy of his thirteenth birthday. His relatively minor summer deceptions hadn't been un-covered, and they certainly weren't hurting anyone. Cromwell was happy. Zach was happy. Kevin's family was happy.

It was happiness all around, basically.

The only aspect of Kevin's life that had become more difficult was the class with Elka. She drove him harder and demanded more than ever—and it's not as if Cromwell were suddenly nailing every training run. In fact, it would be accurate to say that the dog didn't nail *any* training run in the week after the invitational. The dog had improved perceptibly, but he still had only 49.6 seconds of excellence to his credit.

"He will be *splendid* next week," said Elka.

"Really?" asked Kevin. "Because he's not so splen-did this week."

Elka scratched the dog's head. Cromwell slurped her hand.

"Have faith in yourself, Mr. Pugh. And your fine dog."

Faith was nice, but Kevin also wanted preparation on his side. If he and Cromwell were going to embarrass themselves at the United Center, it wasn't going to be the result of any lack of pre-race effort. They ran each day, faithfully.

Kevin also decided that he wouldn't mind some of Elka's spooky mysticism. When she offered him a homemade CD, he dutifully loaded the songs onto his iPod.

"This music will balance and repair you," she said.

"I'm lopsided? I'm broken?" he asked.

"We all have our quirks," Elka said. "You might like the songs, Mr. Pugh."

And so it came to pass that on an idyllic Saturday morning—five days before the Midwest Kennel Club Championship—Kevin raced through Welles Park with Cromwell, listening to what sounded like angry cats being dragged across the strings of a damaged harp.

"This stuff must be . . . (deep breath) . . . kind of an acquired taste," Kevin said to his dog. "But it's probably . . . (deep breath) . . . on top of the charts in . . . (deep breath) . . . well, wherever Elka's from."

Kevin shut down the iPod and went music-less.

He listened to park sounds for a little while—birds in trees, kids on swings, cars honking in streets—and glanced down at his dog. Cromwell had, of course, never been so alert and lively. His tongue flapped, his legs churned. They passed near a dirt field where slovenly men played softball, then another field where small kids played T-ball. Kevin ran hard, and Cromwell kept his pace.

In the distance, Kevin saw a group of kids playing football—there may have been eight of them, or possibly ten. The teams were smallish. It occurred to Kevin that his escape from football camp was easily the strategic highlight of his summer. It had required a flash of inspiration at *just* the right moment, and a coach who gave his full support to an elaborate, unspoken con. Kevin smiled contentedly.

"Tip of the cap . . . (deep breath) . . . to Coach Z," he said. "Without him, Cromwell . . . (deep breath) . . . we wouldn't be where we are today."

As Kevin drew closer to the game, something about the scene became oddly familiar. But he continued the one-sided conversation with his dog.

"In fact . . . (deep breath) . . . I'm willing to say . . . (deep breath) . . . that Coach Z actually saved our sum—"

A voice carried across the field.

"Down! Set!"

Kevin stopped in his tracks, no more than thirty yards from the game.

"Lightning, lightning!"

"No . . . way . . . ," said Kevin softly, squinting.

Cromwell circled him. Clearly, the dog had not wanted to stop.

"*Hut!*" called the voice of the quarterback.

"Okay," said Kevin in a near whisper. "The ball will be snapped, then everyone will chase the quarterback, and then we'll just turn around and go." Cromwell panted. "No one's ever gonna notice us, boy."

But someone already had.

The quarterback was no longer waiting for the snap, and he was no longer barking signals. Instead, he'd taken a few steps toward Kevin. He held a hand over his eyes to block the sun.

"*Pugh?!*" called Brad Ainsworth Jr. "Is that you, Pugh?"

"Oh, hey," replied Kevin, trying desperately to sound casual. "How's it goin'? It's really been a while. Probably haven't seen you since . . . hmm, lemme see . . ."

"Since you broke my face!" called Brad.

"Yeah," said Kevin. "I suppose that would be . . ." Brad was now sprinting toward Kevin.

". . . it."

"*Get him!*" shouted Brad Junior.

"*Go, Crom, go!*" shouted Kevin.

"*Fight!*" shouted several kids, all of whom chased after him.

Kevin chugged across the grass at top speed, and Cromwell raced beside him. It was not at all clear that the dog was aware of any danger in their predicament—Kevin thought he looked happy, in fact. Kevin didn't dare look back at Brad. He just kept sprinting.

He ran across the softball field, cutting between the shortstop and the third baseman. Then he interrupted the T-ball game, scampering over the pitcher's mound.

Parents screamed in disapproval.

"Relax!" he yelled. "There's not even a pitcher!"

Kevin heard Brad's footsteps behind him, but couldn't quite tell where he was. He knew from experience that Brad Junior was ridiculously fast—maybe even Jody/Shasta fast. But he'd never actually been pursued by Brad, because Kevin had never been allowed to touch the ball at camp. Still, they'd established their relative speeds many times, in many ways. All ways ended poorly for Kevin. Based on what he remembered from those horrible mornings at Scherzer, he estimated that he'd be tackled in approximately four seconds . . . three . . . two . . . one . . .

Yet nothing happened.

Kevin and Cromwell kept running.

"Pugh!" cried Brad's voice. "You can't outrun me, Pugh!"

So where the heck are you? thought Kevin.

He eyed the corner of the park nearest to his house, then lowered his head and ran as hard and as furiously as he could.

"Pugh!" screamed Brad.

Kevin and Cromwell kicked up a streak of dirt as they sped across the park.

"Puuuuuugh!"

Each time Brad yelled Kevin's name, it sounded slightly farther away. But that wasn't possible. Kevin needed to sneak a glance, just to know when his doom was at hand. He turned his head slightly, expecting to see Brad just behind him, surrounded by bloodthirsty friends.

Instead, he saw Brad at least forty yards behind—maybe forty-five.

"Hustle up, Ainsworth!" Kevin yelled, smirking.

"You're *dead,* Pugh!" shouted Brad.

Kevin smiled, in spite of his impending deadness. He and Cromwell hauled out of the park, then raced through the neighborhood that separated the park from Kevin's house.

Just a few weeks ago, he thought, *no way would we survive this.*

He peeked at Brad again, who'd fallen farther back. Kevin ran backward for a moment, long enough to yell, "You need me to slow it down, Ainsworth?"

At that point, Brad was no longer responding. He was simply digging in as hard as he could, trying to catch up. A few of his associates seemed to have abandoned the chase, though at least two remained.

Kevin turned and saw his house come into view, then let out a loud, victorious *"Whoooooo!"*

Cromwell woofed. There was no response from Brad Junior.

Kevin hit his driveway at full speed. Not content to simply run inside the house to safely avoid the Brad threat, he ran straight for the Bears Tahoe, jumped onto the hood, and scrambled onto the roof.

There he stood, pumping his fist in triumph, waiting for Brad Junior. Just a few short weeks before, beating any camper in a footrace would have seemed unthinkable. Suddenly Kevin was dusting off the speediest kid he knew.

Cromwell had dashed off into the yard, where he thunked against the tire swing happily.

Several seconds later, Brad finally reached the Pughs' house. He was breathless and accompanied by only one friend—but Brad was no less mad than he'd been at Welles.

"Where've you been, li'l Brad?" said Kevin, pleased with himself. "And what's that on your face?"

Brad Junior wore a clear plastic mask over his nose and eyes.

"I have to wear it now . . . (deep breath) . . . in

sports . . . (deep breath) . . . to protect my nose," managed Brad.

"Ah, gotcha," said Kevin. "You're lookin' good, ace. At least the lisp is gone."

Brad and his friend were bent over, clearly exhausted.

"What the heck . . . (deep breath) . . . are you doing up there, Pugh?" asked Brad.

"I *beat* you!" chirped Kevin. "So I'm celebrating up here. I'm not sure when it happened, li'l Brad, but I'm actually *faster* than you."

He clapped, delighted. Then he broke into a dance sequence—running man, Batsui, moonwalk—and made vague disco sounds atop the Tahoe.

Brad glared, then tapped his friend on the shoulders.

"Pugh," said Junior, "there's still two of us, and one of you. And you're still *dead*."

They began to walk up the driveway—almost zombie-like, but still in pursuit.

"I can run all day," said Kevin happily. He looked down, evaluating potential landing areas and escape routes.

Then the back door opened loudly. Howie Pugh stepped out. Cromwell barked. Howie ran a finger across his mustache and examined the scene.

"Kevin," he said. "Please get off the Tahoe. I just washed it."

"Hey, Dad!" said Kevin cheerfully. "Sure thing."

He looked back at Brad.

"Is that you in the mask there, Ainsworth?" asked Howie.

"Hello, sir," said Brad.

Howie leaned against the doorframe, smiling. "You kids okay out here?"

"We're super!" said Kevin. "We were just having a race. And I *wo*—"

"Your son got kicked out of camp on purpose, Mr. Pugh!" blurted Brad.

Kevin wobbled, like a dazed boxer.

Then his pulse raced. Then he felt breakfast in his throat.

"Wha . . . um . . . wh-wha—" he stammered.

"Bradley," began Howie, not quite patiently. "Kev got expelled from camp for the incident with your face—which was *very* unfortunate and uncalled for. And he's apologized. And he knows it was a cheap sho—"

"It was *not* a cheap shot," said Brad. "It was a total freak accident." Brad glared at Kevin, who was well beyond panicked. "Kevin couldn't hit me if he tr—"

"Okay, then!" said Kevin, hopping down from the Tahoe. "Great seeing you, old camp buddy! Drop by whenever you like."

Kevin walked purposefully toward Brad.

"Kev," said Howie, "I think maybe Bradley is trying to forgive you—albeit in an unusual way. Extend the olive branch, as it were."

"And I will, Dad!" said Kevin anxiously. He turned toward Brad, gripped his shoulders, and tried to steer him toward the street. "Thanks again, bud—"

But Brad wriggled away.

He then delivered a wickedly accurate thirty-second description of Kevin's summer that began with "Coach Zalenski told my dad *everything!*" and ended with "And now Kevin is doing secret dog shows with Zach!"

Kevin stood in the driveway with his mouth agape, stunned.

"What on earth is Bradley *talkin'* about, Kev?" demanded Howie.

Not that it would have helped, but Kevin had no instinct to deny anything. He was awed by Brad—both by his precision and by his ruthlessness.

"H-how . . . ," began Kevin haltingly, ". . . do you even, um . . ."

"How do I know about the dog shows?" asked Brad, with a cold, cruel look on his masked face.

"Y-yeah," replied Kevin, nodding.

"Zach's got video on his blog, champ." Brad winked. Kevin really hated the winking. "Nice little bone trophy, by the way."

Kevin was utterly silent. His mouth still hadn't closed.

"So this nonsense is *true*?!" exclaimed Howie. "Secret dog shows?"

Kevin said nothing. He simply stared at his dad, terrified, sweat streaming down his face.

Brad turned, smiled, and tapped his protective mask with a finger. He patted Kevin's shoulder as he walked by.

"Now we're even, Pugh," he said.

20

Brad's revelations had fallen like little bombs, obliterating several fragile structures that Kevin had built over the course of the summer. The Pugh home became a devastatingly uncomfortable place. When Brad Junior left, Howie simply stood in the yard, clearly dumbfounded, examining his son. At first Kevin said nothing.

He eventually broke the silence by meekly suggesting, "You know, they aren't like dog shows in the traditional sense, Dad."

With that, Howie turned and walked back inside the house, saying nothing in response. He shut the door to his office—which was really more like a small Bears museum—and made three phone calls. The first was to Coach Glussman at Scherzer. There was no need for Kevin to eavesdrop; his dad yelled loud enough to be heard from space. The second call was to Maggie. Their conversation was subdued and serious-sounding. The third call was to Zach's parents. From the other side of the office door, Kevin actually thought that discussion sounded rather pleasant. The only words Kevin heard distinctly were "Apparently Zach is blogging." He couldn't detect any reference to the financial arrangements. There was laughter from Howie, then hushed tones, followed by more (possibly fake) laughing.

Kevin's dad emerged from his office just as grim as he was when he entered. He called for an immediate BFR—his term, referring to a "Big Family Roundtable"—as soon as Maggie and Izzy returned from soccer practice.

"Dad," said Kevin, "I just wanna . . ."

Howie waved a finger.

"Not now, Kev." His mustache quivered.

Kevin shuddered. He squirmed. He could have cried, but instead he went numb and cold until the BFR that afternoon. It was extraordinarily painful for Kevin—and, clearly, for Howie and Maggie.

"Kevin, dear," said his mom, shifting herself in a kitchen chair. "If you didn't want to play football, why say yes to camp?"

Because you asked me in front of live girls, he thought.

"Because Dad basically made me go," he said bitterly.

"*Made* you go!" said Howie, rising. Maggie urged him to sit. He reluctantly obeyed. "Kev, I just presented you with an opportunity..."

"To *what*?! To make a total fool of myself? To do something I've never—not once—expressed the slightest bit of interest in? Ever?"

"As I recall, you came to me to discuss camp options," said Howie.

"No I didn't!" said Kevin, his voice raised nearly to a shriek. "I came to you with a very specific request."

Howie's face scrunched into a knot, then unscrunched.

"You don't even remember?" Kevin pressed. "You know those classes you wouldn't pay for, Dad?"

"You mean the *flute*?" said Howie indignantly. "Is that what this is about? Kevin, we talked about this, it's just not a man's instrument. Your woodwinds are for the ladies, your brass horns and your tubas are for the men—"

"No!" shouted Kevin. "And that was, like, four years ago! I was in third grade!" He shook his head. "And I could have been a good flute player, too."

"Flautist," said Izzy. "They're called flautists, Kev." She put a fresh piece of gum in her mouth.

"Not the point!" declared Kevin. "I was talking about the classes for me and Cromwell, Dad."

Howie raised his eyebrows.

"Oh, right. You mean the ones where I was supposed to *pay* for the dog to do something that he can do in the backyard, for free."

"Yes," said Kevin firmly. "We were having a conversation about me taking classes with Cromwell, and it somehow ended with me in football camp. Without Cromwell. And with Brad."

They all sat quietly for a moment. Then Kevin's mom spoke.

"And these classes with Cromwell . . . these are the dog shows your father mentioned?"

"They're *not* dog shows," Kevin sighed. "And yes, I've been taking classes. That's why I've been jogging. That's where I go three days a week. All summer. No one notices. No one asks."

"So you're taking the doggie classes," said Howie. "How much am I into them for, Kev? Two hundred dollars? Three hun—?"

"You aren't *'into them'* for anything, Dad!"

"Oh, you and Cromwell got a scholarship?" said Howie.

Izzy snorted.

"No," said Kevin. "But I have alternative financing." He sighed. "Zach pays. Cromwell and I train."

Howie looked bewildered.

"I'm not refunding Zachary one cent...," he eventually said, before Maggie interrupted.

"So, Kevin," she said, leaning across the table. "You're taking these dog training classes with Cromwell?"

Cromwell grumbled as he circled Kevin's legs.

"The ones that you and Dad wouldn't pay for, yes."

"Well," began Howie, "I don't think I said we *wouldn't* pay for 'em. I think I said that we ..."

"... would pay for a class that involved 'actual human sports.' " Kevin stared at his dad. "I believe those were your words."

Kevin bent low to pet his dog. Cromwell closed his eyes and made a contented, high-pitched sound.

"Kev," said Howie, "I'm sorry you had to turn to dog shows because you don't feel like we were, you know... *interested* in whatever else you were doing, but..."

"I did not *turn* to anything, Dad," spat Kevin. "People 'turn' to crime, they do not 'turn' to dog shows!" Kevin slid his chair back, exasperated. "And anyway, they're *not* dog shows. It's agility training. A-G-I-L-I-T-Y. Like the sort of thing you need in what you would call 'real sports.' "

"So," said Howie, "you agree that it's not a real sport. It's like a foofy..."

"No, Dad," Kevin sighed. "I don't agree."

Howie opened his mouth, but Kevin cut him off. "Do *not* tell me your ball theory again," he said sternly. "We've been over it, Dad. I understand your position. Soccer is greater than dog agility. Nothing is greater than football. Dog agility is equal to knitting. Or ice dancing. Or ballroom dancing. Believe me, I get it."

Howie said nothing at first, then offered, "Well, ice dancing might be a little extreme, Kev. It's not like that." He sat quietly for just a second. "Unless the dogs wear costumes." Howie thought for a moment, then sat up taller. "These people don't have *you* wearing costumes, right, Kev? Tell me they don't."

Kevin glared at his father.

"Yup, Dad. Frilly costumes. And wigs—fabulous wigs. Makeup, too. And tasteful shoes, with big buckles. It's like a big makeover party every time we ..."

"Kevin!" said his mother abruptly. "You'll give your father a coronary. Enough with the joking."

She settled back into her chair, patting Howie lightly on the arm. His eyes had narrowed and his back had stiffened.

"Honey," said Maggie, "we're very happy that you and Cromwell are enjoying these classes. We think it's great for you to have such a ... well, an active hobby."

Silence.

"Isn't it great, dear?" Maggie said to Howie, tapping him.

And then tapping him harder.

"Yeah, sure, Kev. It really is. Very happy to hear about the hobby. With Cromwell."

Kevin looked at them for a long moment, knowing that his dad regarded agility classes as some sort of illness, one that could be beaten with the appropriate treatment. Which probably involved weightlifting in some way.

"We're good at it, you know," said Kevin. "Dog agility. We win stuff."

He placed their trophy on the table as evidence—he'd retrieved it from his bedroom earlier, in preparation for the BFR.

"Heh!" laughed Howie. "It's a *bone*."

"So cute," said Maggie.

Kevin then explained the exhaustive training that preceded the winning of the cute bone. He raved about Elka, he described the encounter with Jody and Shasta, and he did his best to sell his parents on the significance of the Midwest Kennel Club event.

"It's at the United Center, Dad. Because it's a sport."

Howie stared.

"I thingitz ... (pop) ... totuhwee impwessive ... (crack) ... what you an' Cwomwell're doin'," said Izzy through her gum.

"That's not in dispute," said Howie, his eyes still on the small bronze bone. "No argument here." He stared at Kevin. "It just might be nice if maybe you and the dog would have put your, um ... newfound energy into ..."

"Blocking? Tackling? Passing? Punting?" Kevin smirked.

"No," said Howie. "I mean, not necessarily football. It could be any number of pursuits." He paused, then his eyes locked on Kevin's. "And you know how I feel about *punters,* Kev. The kicking positions aren't for Pughs. That's not to say they aren't important in their own way—"

"What your father would like to say," said Maggie, "is that we're very happy for you and Cromwell."

She smiled.

"But, Kev," said Howie, "you should not have lied to us." Maggie nodded. "And I think you should be grounded."

"What?!" said Kevin, shoving himself away from the kitchen table. "You've *never* grounded me!"

"Well, it never seemed like punishment before," said his dad. "You used to spend all your time in the house anyway. Maybe we coulda grounded you from the basement, but . . ."

"So let me get this straight," said Kevin. "When you thought I'd been expelled from camp for intentionally breaking another kid's face—*breaking his face!*—I wasn't grounded. But now that it turns out it was an accident—and now that I'm good at something that isn't on the approved list of Pugh activities—I'm punished."

He stared at his parents.

"Well, is that right? So you're telling me I can't go to the United Center on Thursday?"

"Yoo can'd punish Cwomwell!" said Izzy, chewing.

"Yeah!" said Kevin. "You'd be punishing the dog!"

"Kevin," said Howie. "You should not have lied to us, period." His nostrils flared and his mustache seemed to fan out. "And for that, you need to . . ."

". . . you need to begin serving your punishment *after* the dog event this week, dear," said Kevin's mom.

Howie spun his head toward Maggie, but she stared him down.

"Your father is right about the lying, of course. There's no place for it in this family, Kevin." She gave her son an unsympathetic look. "We're simply *deferring* your punishment."

Kevin said nothing. They all sat quietly for a few moments. Cromwell barked, and began licking every leg within reach of his tongue.

"Good f'woo, Cwomwell," said Izzy, scratching the dog's nose. Then she removed the gum. "We should all go on Thursday."

"You've got the Under-Eleven Traveling All-Stars Tournament!" said Howie. "And you're *not* missin' it. You've made a commitment to that team."

"I'm still going with Cromwell," said Kevin defiantly.

"Who's gonna take you?" asked Howie.

"Maybe Elka. Maybe Zach's parents. Maybe anyone who realizes it's a big deal."

Howie and Maggie exchanged a look.

Izzy vaulted over the back of her chair and plopped down nimbly on the ground, between Cromwell and her dad. She hugged the dog tightly. Cromwell licked her ear.

"Wish I could be there, Crom," said Izzy, rubbing the dog's fur. "I'm proud of you, boy."

More licking from the dog.

"Are we done?" grumbled Kevin.

Soon he'd retreated to the basement with his dog, his trophy, and the phone. He dialed Zach's cell phone and reached his voice mail.

"This is Z. Leave a message, just for me."

BEEP.

"You uploaded *video*?" said Kevin, still incredulous. "You even put the trophy online? Visible to everyone? *Really?* Smooth move, Zach."

CLICK.

21

The weekend passed. Kevin and Cromwell's Sunday run was notably worse than their Saturday effort. Monday's class at Paw Patch was mostly horrible. No obstacle was safe from Kevin's clumsy feet or from his dog's thrashing tail. Zach met them after class, begging for forgiveness.

"I was just really proud of Team Cromwell, Kev, I swear! No one was supposed to see anything. Honestly, I didn't even know that Zachattack.blogpile.com had readers."

"Well, apparently it does, Webmaster," said Kevin. "But whatever. You're the least of my problems."

They watched Cromwell lunge at the tire swing in the Pughs' backyard. On his best attempts, he scraped rubber and barely squeezed through. On his worst efforts, he nearly knocked himself silly. He was fast, true, but as for his technique regarding obstacles . . . well, it was not exactly refined. And now that Kevin's parents knew about Paw Patch, they were punishing him. Kevin had moved beyond doubt, and was in despair.

On Monday night, he took his familiar seat on the basement couch. No TV, no games. He just sat there. Cromwell was curled in his usual spot. Only a few days earlier, Kevin had been ecstatic and brimming with pride, just like his dog. Now he was crestfallen and the dog was asleep. Their bone-shaped trophy sat between them.

"Crom," he said to his sleeping dog, "I get that we're not supposed to need recognition. I do. We're doing the agility thing for *us*. Because it's fun—at least theoretically. And I understand why I should be able to derive satisfaction from my own—excuse me—from *our* accomplishments. I totally get that, too."

He sighed.

"It would just be nice to have someone else—like, say, Mom and Dad—*watching* us derive satisfaction from our accomplishments. Or at least *want* to watch us. Or at least not ground us for them."

Cromwell grumbled in his sleep.

Kevin sat in silence awhile longer. Eventually, Izzy bounded down the stairs noisily. She dribbled a soccer ball toward Kevin, faked a right-footed kick, and then spun and jabbed the ball past the couch, between two chairs.

"Goooooooaaaallll!" she said in a voice just loud enough to wake the dog.

"Pretty cool about you and Cromwell, Kev," she said, flinging herself onto the couch. Cromwell lifted his head up and licked her, then plopped back down. "Aren't you stoked?"

"I guess," sighed Kevin unstokedly.

"You *guess*? It's not like you two are always bringing home trophies."

She lifted the bone-shaped object and studied it.

"Whatever," said Kevin. "It's shiny. Whoo."

"And Cromwell won it!" said Izzy. She nuzzled the dog's head. "Yes you did, boy, yes you did . . ."

"He *was* pretty awesome." Kevin leaned back.

"You both had to be pretty good, it sounds like."

"I guess."

"You guess a lot, eh?"

They sat quietly for a moment.

"I really do wish I could go on Thursday," Izzy said.

"It's okay." Kevin shrugged. "It's not like I can go to your soccer thing, either."

"Yeah, but you've been to, like, a billion of my soccer games."

"In some pretty awful places," he reminded her.
Izzy grinned.

"Remember that one last winter in . . ."

". . . Champaign?" Izzy said. "Yeah, that was miserable."

"No, I was thinking of the one in . . ."

". . . Ann Arbor? Where the slide at the hotel pool broke? With me on it?"

"Yup, that's the one."

"Yeah, that stunk, too."

Kevin ran his finger down a thick reddish line within the plaid of the couch.

"We won that tournament, though," said his sister.

"You always win, Izzy."

"Nuh-uh," she said, popping off the couch and doing a handstand. "We lost at Grant Park that one time."

"You were six."

"So?"

"So you were playing against nine-year-olds."

"Whatever."

"And they were boys."

She came out of the handstand and hopped back on the couch, then swung her feet atop Kevin's legs.

"Bet you and Cromwell win that thing."

Kevin laughed, somewhat bitterly.

"What's the joke?" asked Izzy.

"First of all, it's kind of a fluke that we've even qualified. Cromwell and I never had a run that was half as good as that one—no, not even a quarter as good. It was insane."

"Dad says that when you do something once, you own it. You have the skill. No one can take it away."

"So?" asked Kevin.

"So as good as you and Cromwell were . . . well, that's how good you *are*. And that's how good you can be again. Whenever. You've just got to . . ."

"Believe? Practice? Visualize? Hustle?" Kevin shook his head. "Right. I've heard the speeches, Iz." Kevin broke into a fair impression of his dad's thick Chicago accent: " 'Repetition, kid. Visualization. *Dat's* da key.' "

She giggled. "It's true."

"I don't even know if we should go on Thursday," Kevin said.

Izzy's mouth fell open and she leapt up from the couch.

"Kevin! You can't *quit*! What about Cromwell?" She stroked the dog's fur. "You have to do it!"

"Well, you're the only one sayin' that in this house. Do you honestly think Mom and Dad give a hoot about the Midwest Whatever-It-Is dog agility championships?" He stared at his sister. "They don't, Iz. They've hardly said a word since the BFR."

"Dad's just got football and radio and stuff. It's Bears training camp time. And we had that soccer thing on the schedule—not that there isn't always soccer on the schedule." She curled herself up and cannonballed back onto the couch. "And I think they're really just total soccer geeks at this point."

"Mom and Dad are total soccer geeks because you *win,* Izzy. You win all the time. You win tournaments, you win MVP awards, you win big giant trophies, not silly little bone-shaped things." Kevin shook his head. "Dad gets to bask in the reflected light of your winner-ness—and he loves it. That's why they're soccer geeks. You *win,* Iz."

"I think they're just soccer geeks because I try."

"Face it, Izzy. You're a winner. I'm really not. I won once, by accident."

"I'm not just some automatic winner, Kevin. I practice, I . . ."

"You win. You're a winner. There are eight hundred awards upstairs to prove it."

"You can't win your eight-hundredth award unless you've won your first." She held up the trophy and smiled. "And you can't win your first if you don't try."

"Trying is *hard,* Iz."

"Success is in the trying, not the triumph."

Kevin stared at her. "Seriously, do you ever run out of Dad's lame clichés?"

Izzy smiled. "When the going gets tough . . ."

". . . the tough use slogans."

Izzy balanced the trophy on her left foot for several seconds, concentrating, then flicked it in the air and caught it. "Anyway," she finally said, "I'm very happy about you and Cromwell."

She skipped upstairs, leaving Kevin to his couch, his exhausted dog, and their trophy.

He would have called Zach to solicit an opinion on participation in the MKC event, but he already knew what Zach would say: Team Cromwell must compete, can't be stopped, rules the universe, has dominion over all dogs, et cetera.

Kevin could confidently say that he had Zach's full support. And Izzy's. They were definitely not the issue.

He tried to watch TV, but failed. Gaming, eating, and, as a last resort, reading all met with similar failure. Eventually, he went upstairs and tried sleep. That did not come easily, either. When it finally did, he dreamt that he was on the asphalt playground of his old elementary school, playing tag, totally unable to touch anyone. He was It, possibly forever. He chased Jody, his sister, Shasta, his father, various characters from cereal ads—Tony the Tiger, the Trix rabbit, Count Chocula—kids from his class, both Brad Ainsworths . . . and Kevin caught none of them, ever.

They claimed various objects as base, then stood and mocked him—stupid base, he thought. Worst part of tag. Count Chocula's comments were particularly stinging: *"Geev up, faht boy,"* he said in that Transylvanian way of his. Elka's voice spat instructions, though Kevin couldn't see her. Cromwell barked, though he, too, was out of sight.

Kevin woke up sweat-drenched and breathless, his heart racing. He checked his surroundings, slowly recognizing that he was not actually trapped in a game of unwinnable tag. He was in his room. It was still completely dark outside. No moonlight, no sound.

Kevin eyed his clock: 3:59.

Then it flipped to 4:00.

Kevin looked down to the foot of his bed. Cromwell was staring back at him.

"You think our agility careers just peaked, boy?"

They stared at one another for a long moment, locked in some sort of nonverbal but not meaningless dialogue.

"No, me neither."

And then Kevin swept the covers off the bed, adjusted his pajamas, yawned, and said, "Okay, Crom, let's go."

The dog hopped off the bed as though he were dismounting an apparatus. Then he led the way through the hall, down the stairs, and into the backyard in the pitch-black predawn. Kevin flipped on an outdoor floodlight, illuminating the yard.

Cromwell bounced up and down anxiously. He whined, and Kevin shushed him.

Then Kevin dragged several old toys from the garage, arranging them—along with patio furniture and a few lawn-care implements—into a suitable obstacle course for the dog. He and Cromwell ran the makeshift course repeatedly over the next ninety minutes, Kevin urging his dog along in a whisper. He extracted Cromwell from the tire swing at least half a dozen times.

Had he ever looked up toward his sister's bedroom window, he might have seen her nose pressed against it while she watched her brother down below.

22

After returning to bed just after 5:30 a.m., Kevin slept soundly. When he blinked his eyes open again, the bedroom clock said 10:49.

He wiped the sleep from his eyes, yawned, stretched, jostled his dog awake, and both plodded out into the hallway and stumbled sleepily downstairs. Kevin stopped halfway down the steps when he heard the voices of Izzy and his dad below. Izzy was using her on-field voice. Normally those two just used sports references and told each other unfunny jokes. They didn't argue, ever.

Until that morning.

Kevin sat on the stairs, listening, with Cromwell on his lap.

"One time!" said Izzy. "I just mean one lousy

time—one lousy game that they can probably win anyway."

"Iz, this is crazy," said Howie. "And I wouldn't expect it from you. I thought you were serious about the soccer."

"I *am* serious!" she declared. "But how often do Kevin and Cromwell have something this important?"

"Now you're making *my* point," said Howie, slurping what Kevin suspected was milk from a cereal bowl. "For you, soccer is a long-term commitment, Iz. And when you commit to a thing like that—more importantly, when you commit to a *team*—you honor the commitment." He paused. "You honor it every day. Not just when it's convenient."

"But . . ."

"That's like a sacred commitment you have to the Under-Eleven All-Stars, kid. *Sacred.* A bond forged in blood and tears. Like with warriors. You're comrades in battle, everyone doing their . . ."

Kevin heard his mom laugh.

"There's been no bleeding, dear," she said. "Or swords, or weapons of any kind. You're laying it on a little thick."

Thank you, Mom.

"It's a metaphor," said Howie. "And a very popular one. War and sports—I didn't make this up. Izzy, these kids you'll be facing at that tournament . . . well, they're the best U-11's from a six-state area. The most talented kids in the region. That's a big deal. If you want to be the best, you gotta beat the best."

Kevin smirked, recalling that his financier had said the same thing. Howie continued.

"And if you want to *beat* the best, you have to face 'em, kid. You never duck a challenge."

"But wouldn't the same thing apply to Kevin and Cromwell?" asked Izzy.

"A fair point," said Maggie.

Yeah! thought Kevin, the stair creaking slightly beneath him. *Tell it, ladies.*

"No, actually," said Howie. "It's different with dogs, hon."

Kevin's shoulders dropped.

"How could it be different with dogs?" protested Izzy.

"Different species, Iz. More legs. Different rules. Like for instance, there's no Ditka equivalent in the dog world. It's just different." He chewed a mouthful of cereal. Kevin could hear his spoon clanking against the bowl.

"How does Coach Ditka have any—?" began Izzy.

"And besides," continued her dad, "no disrespect intended to Cromwell, but, well . . . c'mon. You've spent your whole life working toward . . ."

"I'm ten, Dad. My whole life is ten years long. Let's not get carried away."

Cromwell works hard, too, Dad.

"And you've spent most of those ten years working really hard at soccer. Every day, kicking in the backyard, at the park, in the basement. Nerf balls, rubber balls, regulation balls. Dribbling, kicking, shooting, passing . . . every day. Your mother and I have been there with you, too, kid." He chewed a little more, then continued. "How long have Cromwell and Kevin spent with the dog training? A month?"

"But it's in *dog* months," said Izzy. "So they're longer. One month for a human is like seven months for a dog, I think. We're talking about a big chunk of Crom's life here, Dad."

Oh. That's kinda dark. Kevin reflexively shielded Cromwell's ears.

"Be that as it may," said Howie, "for Kevin it's still only been a month. That's not the same kinda commitment you have. Not at all . . . not even close, in fact."

Izzy didn't respond.

Kevin slumped back against the stairs. *How can I reason with that?*

Cromwell wagged his tail, oblivious to the details of the conversation below.

"And I'll tell you another thing," said Howie, his voice rising slightly. "Kevin didn't even tell his mother and me about these dog show classes."

"It's dog *agility*," Maggie reminded him. "Not dog

show. We've been corrected on this point before, and it really gets to Kevin. So please remember: *agility.*"

"Well, how would we know?" demanded Howie. "Kevin hid it from us all this time!"

"He tried to ask you," said Izzy. "Remember, he wanted to take the classes; you said . . ."

"I said I wouldn't *pay* for 'em, not until Kevin could convince me of the practical benefits." More muffled crunching sounds. "Or until he could convince me that he was serious about it. But did we hear another word?" Crunch, crunch. "No." Crunch, crunch. "Not until little Bradley Ainsworth spilled his guts."

"The little rat," said Izzy.

"A rat he may be," said Howie, "but Kevin should've told us everything."

"But don't you see how serious he is now?" asked Izzy.

Howie said nothing. He simply chewed.

"It just doesn't seem fair," Izzy continued. "Not fair at all. Kevin has gone to so many of my tournaments. And he gets bored out of his mind."

Kevin nodded.

"Oh, they're like little mini-vacations for us all," said Maggie. "Don't be silly."

"I'd just like to be there for Kev and Cromwell, that's all."

"And that's a lovely sentiment," said Howie, rising and pushing in his chair noisily. "But I can't let you quit on that team, Iz. Not *that* team, and not *any* team." Howie jingled his keys. "We are not a family that quits, period. And besides—again, no disrespect to Cromwell here, because I respect what you're doing—but you've got a chance to go all the way, kid. You're gonna win that thing. Kev didn't really seem too confident about his chances this Thursday."

With that, Kevin's eyes widened. He absently slipped down a step, thumping on the staircase. His family below seemed oblivious to the sound.

"Okay," said his dad. "Gotta go. Big interview day today. Probably won't be back till late."

The back door opened and closed. Howie left the house whistling.

Kevin sat just below the middle step, his chin resting in his hands, his dog sitting behind him. Cromwell licked Kevin's elbow.

Not that winning matters, Kevin thought. *Not to Howie Pugh.*

He sat up, nudged his dog, and quietly went back upstairs.

23

The Midwest Kennel Club Championship crept up on Kevin, like a stealthy ninja. Kevin and Cromwell had yet another not-entirely-successful day of training with Elka. They never managed to complete her course in anything less than 52 seconds—and that was before various infractions were factored into their time. Elka remained patient, though Kevin couldn't figure out why or how. At home, all the little 0:00:49.600's he'd doodled seemed to mock him.

Elka dropped by the Pugh home unannounced on Wednesday night.

"I would like to confirm that you have these parents that are often referred to, yet never seen," she told Kevin at the door. He sighed, reluctantly allowing her inside.

Howie and Maggie Pugh were pleasant enough with Elka, though Kevin's dad was always visibly suspicious of people who hadn't heard of him.

"You know," said Elka, "Kevin and Cromwell's achievement is *exceptional,* given their very limited experience and training."

"Which is, like, a month, right?" asked Howie.

"Yes, Mr. Pugh."

"Because it seems like just yesterday that Cromwell was a piece of furniture."

"He is now an elite athlete," said Elka, scratching Cromwell's head.

"Hmm," said Howie. "What's that make Kevin, then?"

"Whatever he chooses," said Elka. "He has been tremendous."

Kevin blushed, though he wasn't feeling especially tremendous at the time.

Elka spent several minutes explaining the changes she felt Cromwell and Kevin had undergone over the summer—mostly physical for the dog, physical and perhaps mental for Kevin.

"The boy who came to me earlier this summer could never have successfully led such a marvelous dog as Cromwell. But Kevin has grown quite a lot."

"Looks to me," said Howie, "like he's actually ungrown. He's shed some weight." Howie looked at his son. "You've lost your foundation, kid."

"Mr. Pugh," said Elka, "Kevin will need to be in the best possible condition for tomorrow's championship—physically, mentally, emotionally. This is a very demanding event, sir."

"I thought the dogs did the running," said Maggie.

"The dog will go as far as Kevin takes him."

Kevin went to bed on Wednesday feeling incapable of taking Cromwell anywhere. After a fitful night's sleep, he awoke on Thursday to his obnoxious alarm. He blinked his eyes open and considered simply calling Elka, feigning illness. The MKCC was going to end poorly—that much he absolutely knew.

Then Kevin realized that Elka was already in the Pughs' driveway, honking the horn of an ancient Volkswagen.

"Let's *go*, Team Cromwell!" cried Zach from the passenger seat of Elka's car.

Kevin buried his head in his pillow.

Cromwell sniffed at him, then licked him frantically until he got out of bed.

Kevin had actually attended only five events at the United Center. Three of those events were circuses, another was a Bulls game—more accurately, three-quarters of a Bulls game, before he threw up an Italian beef all over his dad's pants—and the fifth was *Monsters Inc. on Ice*. Kevin had only truly enjoyed that last one. He had a weakness for ice-skating productions, though he didn't dare reveal it to his family.

Elka drove Kevin, Zach, and Cromwell to the stadium long before the event was scheduled to start.

"This car smells like hamster," Zach whispered to Kevin, a little too loudly.

"This car," said Elka, "has weathered many things, Zachary."

Cromwell hopped from lap to lap excitedly during the drive.

"Sorry your parents can't see Team Cromwell today," said Zach.

"Yeah, well . . . they're with Team Izzy today. Not the first time, won't be the last."

Elka parked in a lot that was designated for participants, then entered the stadium through a gate at the northeast corner. A sign above it read MKCC MEDIA & COMPETITORS' ENTRANCE.

"Media?" asked Kevin.

"I believe I told you that it was an event with some prestige," answered Elka.

Once they were inside, the enormity of the place seemed to shrink them. Kevin felt surges of nervousness. Cromwell zigzagged as they walked down the wide corridors, barking and whining at seemingly every animal they passed—and many of the animals they passed were, in Elka's words, "most irregular."

There were dogs receiving massages from accredited specialists.

There was a team of dogs and handlers wearing faux-leather jackets and studded collars.

There were dogs in bejeweled carrying cases; dogs wearing capes, tiaras, leopard-skin outfits, bow ties, tiny mirrored sunglasses, Star Wars costumes— mostly shih-tzus dressed as Ewoks, but also one Chewbacca, one Yoda, and at least three Leias— military uniforms, business suits, bunny ears, Mohawks, and fairy wings; and several different breeds wearing fancy hats.

A particularly yappy corgi and its middle-aged male handler wore matching satin tops. The dog's tight-fitting shirt had white lettering that read BAD 2 THE BONE. The man's tight-fitting shirt had lettering that read BRAD 2 THE BONE. They made eye contact with no one.

"Dude, that could *totally* be Team Cromwell," said Zach. "But maybe not so shiny. And not taupe, but . . ."

"But teal?" asked Kevin.

"Right. Team colors."

Cromwell was clearly skittish.

There were hundreds of displays run by aggressive salespeople hawking products for dogs and dog lovers. Zach dutifully gathered business cards.

"Just in case Cromwell achieves the stardom I've foreseen . . . and you *fear*," he told Kevin. "These jokers will crawl to us, begging for product endorsements."

"Right. Cromwell Pugh, superstar celebrity pitch-dog."

"Kids will want officially licensed gear from Team Cromwell," continued Zach, taking out a video camera. "Lunch boxes, video games, energy drinks. We're an agility powerhouse. As your business manager, I'm just performing due diligence."

"No video today," said Kevin.

"Come *on*!" said Zach. "Just for my personal coll—"

"No . . . video . . . today," repeated Kevin.

Cromwell strained at his leash and whined as he wove through the legs of passersby on the way to the check-in area.

"Dude, calm the talent," said Zach, watching Cromwell flit around on his leash, constantly tangling and untangling himself. "The dog must chill."

"The dog is freaked," said Kevin. "The handler is freaked. We're just generally—"

Zach stopped abruptly and pointed down the corridor—at a Doberman wearing a dog-sized Bears jersey with PUGH 56 on the back.

"Oh, man," said Zach. "That is so . . ."

". . . totally unexpected," said Elka. "Your marketing efforts appear to have paid off, Zachary."

Kevin laughed.

"That's my dad's jersey," he said.

"Your father makes dog jerseys?" asked Elka.

More laughter.

"No, he's just . . . well, he played football. People know him. He was a Bear."

"And I was a stewardess," said Elka. "But that was a long time ago."

She made a disgusted face as they passed the dog in the Pugh jersey. Elka took the leash from Kevin, bent low, then scooped up Cromwell in her right arm. He licked her and sniffed; she lifted his ear and muttered unintelligible things into it. Then she addressed the boys.

"Let me teach you something about dogs," she said, walking fast. "They were domesticated from wolves, probably in East Asia, and almost certainly 15,000 years ago." Cromwell licked her again. "For the next 14,990 years, they were naked—totally naked. They wore nothing but their own fur. No holiday sweaters, no tracksuits, no hats." She swept her left hand across the spectacle of costumed dogs. "And now look at them. People dressing them like little Kens and Barbies." She eyed Zach. "Please do not put one of your little uniforms on Cromwell. He neither needs nor wants it, Zachary."

Elka set Cromwell down on the slick floor, and he fell in stride with her.

"So Cromwell was a wolf?" asked Kevin, watching his small, roundish, droopy-eared dog trundle along.

"Thousands of years ago, Mr. Pugh. His forebears were wolves. Dogs were domesticated from them to protect us."

Kevin could not imagine Cromwell as either a wolf or a protector of anything, except possibly chew toys—and he'd give up a chew toy if you offered him something chicken-flavored or bacon-scented.

To Elka, dogs in tracksuits and handlers in matching outfits may have appeared silly. But they all seemed to be eyeing Kevin and Cromwell sharply, sizing them up, looking for weakness.

Kevin certainly had plenty of weakness to offer.

24

Elka checked them in, received all their race materials, and then mingled with various trainers and agility enthusiasts. Kevin tried to ignore the other dogs and their handlers as best he could, but Zach was not much help in this regard. He kept pointing out tough-looking animals and their intimidating owners.

Still, Kevin tried to keep his mind on Cromwell and the course—just the course.

Don't even consider the competition, he told himself. *They aren't the obstacles. We don't climb them. We don't jump them. Don't let them distract you.*

Whenever Kevin was able to direct his focus away from the other dogs, it was soon redirected to the stands. The Midwest Kennel Club event apparently attracted a crowd of actual *paying* customers—not a large crowd by the arena's standards, but large enough to fill much of the stadium's first level.

And this audience—which Zach excitedly estimated to be three thousand or so people—did nothing for Kevin's self-confidence. As soon as Elka strayed, Cromwell seemed to come unglued, too. The television crews certainly didn't help.

"Come *on*!" said Zach. "A crowd is a *good* thing. I've heard athletes discuss this. They feed off the crowd's energy. At least I think that's what they say. So try feeding—that's never been a problem for you before."

"Funny stuff," said Kevin, his eyes sweeping across the stands. "I don't think I'm the feed-off-the-crowd sort of athlete. In fact, I don't actually feel like I'm any kind of athlete."

Zach rubbed Kevin's shoulders vigorously, like a boxing trainer with a fighter.

"You are one-half of an award-winning dog agility machine, dude. And you're not even the *dog* half. Cromwell does the tricks . . . what the heck can go wrong?"

Plenty, it turned out.

During their preliminary walk-through, all of Cromwell's old problems returned. It was like their first week at Paw Patch all over again. The dog was leaping too soon from the ramps and the seesaw; he missed weave poles; he brushed against hurdles; and, of course, he whacked himself silly with the bottom of the suspended hoop.

From the edges of the course, competitors snickered as the unknown boy-and-dog combo botched pretty much every apparatus.

As Cromwell crossed the seesaw, Kevin slipped, flailed, and then landed facedown on the green turf. His belly hit the opposite end of the seesaw that Cromwell was on, catapulting the dog into a low trajectory.

The crowd of onlookers issued a collective *"Ooooh!"*

The dog bayed an abrupt *"Rrooooo!"*

Cromwell hit the turf rather gracefully, rolled a few times, then shook himself off and ran back to Kevin, drooling. Kevin didn't want to pick his head up. His fall—and Cromwell's flight—was shown in slow motion on the giant scoreboard suspended above the United Center floor.

And then it was shown again.

And again, even slower, this time focusing on Kevin's pained expression.

Each time it was shown, the accompanying laughter seemed to grow louder.

Finally, the scoreboard switched to something

else . . . Jody and Shasta. The girl was laughing, no doubt at the image she'd just seen of a stumbling, awkward Kevin Pugh. Or, as she had pronounced it, "Poo."

But as her face appeared on the scoreboard, many in the crowd began to respectfully cheer. She switched from laughter to the too-polite, too-obnoxiously-sweet wave she'd delivered at Paw Patch. Kevin trudged off the course, his chin down, his feet shuffling slowly. It was unusually cold on the floor of the arena. The United Center was colossally large, full of echoes and vast distances. The atmosphere was disconcerting, really.

"That did not go well, Mr. Pugh," said Elka as her protégé left the course.

"Oh really?" said Kevin sarcastically. "Hmm. Well, you're the expert, I suppose. What clued you in? Was it the first time you saw the video of me falling, or the third?"

"This is not the best day for the dour, self-defeating Kevin Pugh to return," Elka said quietly. "Nor for the wilder, undisciplined Cromwell."

Kevin knew that much was true, but he wasn't sure how to make either of them go away. He decided to walk off his nerves, if possible. But as he circled the arena, the walk only reminded him of the presence of other people—*many* other people.

"Almost showtime," said Zach when Kevin returned. Zach was nervously tapping a foot and looking into the faces of the crowd. "You know, I might have underestimated the size of the audi—"

"Okay, shut up," snapped Kevin. "Not helpful, dude. Not in any way helpful."

"Sor-*ry*," said Zach. "Just a little uptight, I guess." Kevin flashed a very ticked-off look.

"Not for any, um . . . particular reason," said Zach. "Certainly not because of, um . . . that warm-up. Which really wasn't so ba—"

"Okay, really. Shut"—Kevin held his right hand in front of his mouth and made a zipping motion—"up. There will be no more talking among Team Cromwell. None. Total silence. This has not been one of your better pep talks, so let's just cut our losses."

Zach slouched into one of the folding chairs that ringed the course. Kevin sat down next to him and waited quietly. He watched as Elka shared one of those odd, indecipherable conversations with his dog, lifting his ears, whispering secrets to Cromwell that were apparently quite reassuring. The dog panted happily.

At that moment, Kevin needed some reassurance himself, and Zach clearly wasn't going to provide it. None of the voices in Kevin's head were especially positive:

"Kev didn't really seem too confident about his chances"... *"Of course you were both technically horrible"*... *"These people don't have you wearing costumes, right, Kev?"*... *"I had not imagined that Cromwell could be ready for an event of this magnitude"*...

A summer's worth of discouragement drifted through Kevin's mind. He tried thinking of the little motivational phrases that his dad was always offering Izzy, but he kept mixing them together in a stew of total sports gibberish: "Give 110 percent of want it more to the next level of gut-check time to get no respect..."

"WELCOME!" said a booming public-address voice, jarring Kevin from his self-obsession. From floor level, the voice sounded as if it belonged to some evil cartoon super-villain. Kevin fussed, but Cromwell remained stone-still.

"The Midwest Kennel Club is pleased to welcome you to its thirty-third annual agility championships, here at the United Center!" The crowd of thousands roared, then stood for the national anthem.

Dogs soon began racing through the course... *fast.*

It was clear that whatever spaz/speed advantage Cromwell enjoyed at Paw Patch was more than matched here among the region's very best dogs. Cromwell, with Elka lightly stroking his head, appeared at ease—for the moment. Yet as each new dog raced through the event with another sub-50-second time, Kevin felt less confident and more panicky. He couldn't tune out the words of discouragement and dismissal floating in his head.

The dogs kept coming, and they were all, it seemed, spectacular. Elka applauded each one. Few penalties were enforced, and all the dogs, regardless of breed or handler, seemed to be stars.

Not surprisingly, given their usual lack of luck, Kevin and Cromwell were going to have to wait through every performance before they would get their opportunity—or, as seemed more accurate, their comeuppance. They were scheduled to go last. As new times were posted—0:00:48.600 . . . 0:00:49.700 . . . 0:00:46.100—Kevin saw just how far from ready he and Cromwell were for this. Elka's original instinct about them had been correct.

He looked into the stands and saw the faces of the dog enthusiasts, then assessed the crowd of animals and handlers.

Dad's totally right, thought Kevin. *This is a silly event made up by a bunch of losers who are just too lame to compete in real sports—and I'm not even good enough for it.*

After twenty-nine other pairs had performed, Jody's and Shasta's names were announced.

Cheers arose and cameras flashed throughout the arena.

The reigning champs smiled at the crowd. Then,

as they reached the starter's line, they struck a dead-serious pose.

"She certainly is a single-minded little person," said Elka.

"Freak show," said Zach.

"Cold-blooded assassin," said Kevin, the first words he'd uttered in perhaps an hour. He shook his head.

"Mr. Pugh," began Elka, "you are not to concern yourself..."

"...with the other handlers and their dogs. Right. Gotcha. Hadn't given 'em a thought."

Cromwell seemed to be watching the overhead scoreboard rather intently.

Jody and Shasta were like a special ops team. They moved at inhuman speed and with ruthless efficiency, wasting no steps. The dog barely seemed to make contact with any surfaces; it soared gracefully over each impediment. The girl made no unnecessary movements whatsoever.

She might be a two-faced little cretin, thought Kevin, *but she's kind of a badass dog handler.*

Ramp, hurdle, tunnel, hurdle, wall, tube, table, weave, seesaw, hoop . . . finished.

The digital clock flashed 0:00:40.100.

The crowd exploded.

"Yeesh!" said Zach.

Elka stood and clapped.

"And that is a new Midwest Kennel Club record!" bellowed the P.A. announcer.

Cromwell turned his head and studied his owner.

In a quick, decisive motion, Kevin Pugh slipped the leash onto his dog's collar and got to his feet.

"Come on, Cromwell," he said. "We're outta here."

25

Elka and Zach pursued Kevin down the long gray arena corridor and up the short flight of stairs that led to Madison Street. Zach tugged at Kevin's arm, begging him to turn around. But Kevin shrugged him off like a gnat and stomped ahead. Cromwell whimpered, clearly not pleased to have moved so far away from the agility course.

"Do *something*, Ms. Brandt!" yelled Zach. "You can't just let this chucklehead break up Team Cromwell! Not like this, not now! I have plans for us! Merchandi—!"

"Zachary," she said, "the chucklehead may do as he pleases. I have never once forced a pupil onto a course, and I will not do it today."

Kevin stopped near the Michael Jordan statue at the arena's east entrance and looked back at Elka.

"I'm sorry," he said. "I really am. I'm sorry, Zach; I'm sorry, Cromwell; and I'm sorry, Elka." He looked at the ground. "I thought I was ready for . . . no, I thought I *wanted* this, but . . ."

"But you do not?" asked Elka.

Kevin was silent.

"Of course he wants it!" shouted Zach. "He's trained for weeks! Like, really trained! Eating icky food, exercising, practicing, more exercise, more practicing . . . and for *what*? To give up? When he gets to the highest level of competi—!"

"This isn't even the highest level, dude. There's always another level. You win the Midwest, you go to the nationals. . . . You win the nationals, you go to the *inter*nationals. . . . You win those, you go to the inter*planetary*. . . . it doesn't end. It never ends!"

"Until today," said Zach angrily.

"Until today," said Kevin flatly.

"You wish to go home, then, Mr. Pugh?"

"Yeah," said Kevin, looking away. Cromwell whimpered again.

"And you are sure?"

"I'm rarely this sure of anything."

Zach stomped back toward the arena's entrance. "I'll catch the bus," he muttered.

"C'mon, dude," called Kevin. "Do you even have money for the bus?"

"I was the *financier*!" shouted Zach. "Of course I have money for the bus."

Kevin noticed Elka smiling at Zach, just for an instant. And then her expression flattened.

"So shall we go?" she asked.

"Uh-huh," he said.

Cromwell took several steps toward Zach, whining a bit more, and Kevin scooped his dog up into his arms. He felt a great rush of guilt, knowing that his dog shared none of his reservations. "Sorry, boy," he said. "I really am." There was no licking. Just staring. "It was all fun while it lasted, Cromwell—really fun. You were awesome. The best. But we've done all we . . ."

Suddenly Kevin heard the familiar tones of "The Super Bowl Shuffle" via car horn.

Kevin's head snapped up as the Pughs' Tahoe screeched to a halt mere feet from the Jordan statue. Izzy hopped out through a rear window without opening the door.

Ignoring her mother's yelling, she raced toward Kevin and Cromwell, hugged them, and chirped, "Whashup, bro?" She cracked her gum.

Kevin simply stared.

Howie and Maggie exited the SUV with looks of grave concern on their faces.

"Did we *miss* it?" Howie asked Elka. "We couldn't

have missed it! I *just* called! I said, 'Hey, did the Pugh kid go yet?' They said, 'No, he's up in fifteen or twenty minutes.' I said, 'That's grea—' "

"What are you guys *doing* here?" Kevin asked incredulously.

"We're here to see the big dog show!" said Maggie. Everyone stared at her. "I mean the agility competition," she said quickly. "Not a dog show, which is something very different."

A United Center security guard approached and began to speak.

"Sir, I'm afraid you can't park your car here, not by the . . . oh, *dang!* You're Howie Pugh, ain't you?"

An autograph and two pictures later, they were legally parked.

"So you blew off Izzy's game?" Kevin asked.

"We skunked 'em," Izzy said, hopping up and down and removing the wad of gum. "Mercy rule. Ten-nothin', Team Illinois beats Team Wisconsin. It was a rout. Fifteen minutes, tops. Slaughter rule invoked. Game over."

Cromwell licked Izzy's hand.

"That's, um . . . that's cool that your team mercied 'em, I guess."

"Not her *team*," said Maggie. "Izzy actually mercied them."

"Nine goals," said Kevin's sister, raising her hand

slightly. "One assist. Boom, boom, boom, boom, boom . . . ," she said, making a series of phantom kicks. "A great team effort. We skipped the trophy thing—who needs another?—and hit the road."

Izzy smiled.

"Dad," said Kevin, "this really isn't necessary. I mean . . ."

"I thought you'd be happy we were here," said Howie.

Kevin was, actually. He was delighted, in fact. He was also standing outside with the dog in his arms, headed to Elka's car.

The trainer smiled at him.

"Is there something you would perhaps like to say to your family, Kevin?" she asked.

But he was dumbfounded.

"I think maybe *I* should start," said Howie, leaning a hand against the base of the statue. "And I should start by saying that I was an idiot, Kev. And a baby." He paused. "I was an idiot-baby, basically." He rubbed his hands together, appearing to search for words. "If I'm gonna teach you anything about commitment and effort, you need to know that I'm *completely* committed to you. Win or lose. Football or . . . um . . . dog." He shuffled his feet. "Look, we want you to find what you love, and then do it—really do it. If you and Cromwell are as great as we hear, we'd all love to watch you."

228

Howie looked at his son earnestly.

"And if you're *not* as great as everyone says, that's okay, too. It's not important where you finish. All that matters is what you give."

Kevin stared at his father, stunned.

"Um . . . thanks," he finally said. "W-we give, um . . . a lot."

Cromwell whimpered again.

"So did we miss it?" asked Maggie. "Because your father really did call, and they really did say . . ."

"Oh, no," said Kevin. "You're totally on time. We were just, um . . ."

"A pep talk," said Elka, discreetly tucking her car keys back into her bag. "I always insist on a quick outdoor pep talk before Kevin takes the course."

"Yeah?" asked Howie, eyeing Elka.

"A Paw Patch tradition," she said.

"And you just missed the pep talk, Dad," said Kevin. "Sorry."

"Let me tell ya, Kev," said Howie, with a fiery look in his eye, "I've heard pep talks from the best of the pep-talkers. I've been in the presence of motivational geniuses. Gifted orators. I once saw my defensive co-ordinator take a machete to a life-sized mannequin that was dressed like a Lions quarterback."

Kevin saw Elka's eyes widen.

"Yeah," Howie said, "that story doesn't always go

over well in the retelling. People hear 'machete' and they just assume it was gross. But it was really very stirring. Very little gore. Men wept."

."Had to be there, I guess," said Kevin.

"That's my point!" continued his dad, "You gotta be there, Kev! Like you and Cromwell are *here*." Howie pointed at the arena. "This is no practice field, Kev. It's the UC. You only get to compete in a building like this if you put the work in. Getting here is the big thing." He paused. "It's not the minutes on the course we'll be cheering for, kid. It's the hours of work we didn't see. No matter where you finish, you've really impressed us."

"And we're proud," said Maggie.

Howie smiled.

"Yes we are," he added. "And I've always thought that if you work like a dog in practi . . . oh, no offense intended there, Cromwell. It's an expression. If you work *hard* in practice, then the games are nothin'. They're like a party."

He gripped Kevin's shoulders.

"This is the fun part," Howie said. "You ready, Kev?"

"Um, I mean . . . well, I like parties . . ."

Howie squeezed Kevin's shoulders tighter, then looked at the dog. Cromwell was fidgeting wildly, whirring like a kitchen gadget.

"Your partner is definitely ready."

Kevin looked at the eager dog, the grinning family, and the unusually calm Elka, and he decided that he was ready, too.

"Let's do this thing," he said firmly.

"You are certain, Mr. Pugh?" asked Elka.

But Kevin had already dropped the dog and begun to sprint toward the doors, Cromwell at his heels. Soon the entire family was running through the competitors' entrance—thanks to the Bears-loving security guard—down a flight of stairs, and back into the chilly United Center corridors.

Kevin focused on his dad's words: "If you work hard in practice, then the games are nothin'."

Yeah, he thought. *This is nothin'. The fun part.*

He looked down at his excited, wide-eyed dog. This was clearly fun for him. Cromwell barked and wove his way through the crowd of competitors, handlers, and members of the media, clearing a path for the family. Re-energized, Kevin streaked past other competitors, not bothering to make eye contact. He knew—or at least suspected—that they were smirking at the boy who'd nearly knocked himself unconscious on the seesaw. But he didn't care.

Kevin spied Zach in a corner, still clearly angry, stuffing a few belongings into his backpack. He'd already removed his Team Cromwell jersey.

Kevin darted over to him, tapped him on the shoulder, and breathlessly said, "Game on."

"Wha—?" said a clearly befuddled Zach. "You're in, you're out. The game's off, it's on . . ."

"No," said Kevin urgently, "it's *so* on."

Cromwell woofed, then pressed a paw on Zach's foot, then barked again.

The P.A. announcer called Kevin and his dog to the course.

"Get that jersey back on," said Kevin, whacking Zach's backpack.

26

Elka gripped Kevin's hand and smiled as the announcer called his name. The hum of the crowd was constant, and the lights were harsh. A ring of flickering advertisements littered the floor. The air smelled like stale popcorn and nacho cheese, with just a hint of dog poop. Kevin grinned confidently. Elka's bracelets jangled.

"Don't you have anything to say to Cromwell?" Kevin asked. "In your secret dog-speak?"

"Cromwell is perfectly prepared," Elka answered, smiling wider. "And this has already been a most successful day for you, Mr. Pugh."

"Thanks."

Kevin and Cromwell hurried to the course, walking perfectly in step with one another. They were followed closely by Zach, who was back in his teal Team Cromwell jersey.

"This is gonna be awesome, Kev," said Zach. "Just promise me you won't spaz—"

"Dude," said Kevin. "I did *not* come back for another of your motivational talks."

"Sorry. Right. I'll, um . . ."

"You'll enjoy the performance of Team Cromwell, for better or worse."

The three of them brushed past Jody and Shasta, who were preparing to be interviewed by a WFRK reporter. The terrier yapped happily at Cromwell. But Cromwell did not turn around. He stared intently at the course ahead.

"Oh, are you still *here?*" the black-haired girl asked, smirking. Kevin froze. "I thought I saw you leave," she continued. "We all thought maybe you hurt yourself. You know, falling on your face. In front of everyone. The seesaw can be so cruel." She grinned.

Kevin smiled back, which seemed to unnerve her a bit.

"If the worst thing that ever happens to me occurs on a seesaw," he said, "then I'm probably doing okay."

The WFRK reporter jabbed a microphone into the girl's face and began talking.

"That's right, Brad, I'm here with world-renowned MKC dog agility champion Shasta Gatkowski and her dog, Jody . . ."

"The *dog* is named Jody and the *chick* is Shasta?" blurted Zach, just loud enough to be heard by WFRK viewers. "No way!"

Zach laughed, drawing an angry look from a producer and a sharp glance from the reporter.

Kevin stepped toward the starting line with Cromwell, and a Midwest Kennel Club representative greeted them. The stands had emptied somewhat—not that Kevin was thinking about any audience members other than the assembled Pughs and Zach and Elka.

Cromwell stood rigid and steely-eyed at the starting line. Elka was right. He was ready.

Kevin and his dog shared another determined look. Kevin nodded. Cromwell grumbled, low and purposefully. The buzz in the arena melted away to a soft, indistinct murmur.

The kennel club representative stepped away from the starting line.

"You may begin whenever you are . . ."

"GO!" shouted Kevin.

". . . ready."

Cromwell's explosion off the line drew a gasp from the crowd.

Cromwell zipped up, down, over, and through, almost as though he weren't bound by the laws of ordinary physics. The ramps, the hurdles, the tunnels, and the walls were all conquered as if they weren't even there, weren't obstacles at all.

Kevin moved with precision and shocking quickness. Zach was hooting wildly, only four feet from the live WFRK interview. The reporter was powerless to stop him. Shasta was clearly disturbed, sputtering into the microphone, cringing whenever Zach yelled.

Elka, Howie, Izzy, and Maggie inched toward the course.

"That's my boy!" bellowed Howie.

"And our dog!" shouted Maggie.

Cromwell nailed all the necessary points of contact on the seesaw. Only the hoop remained.

Kevin sprinted hard, just ahead of his dog.

"Wait . . . wait . . . wait . . . ," he said, just as he had before. *BOOM!*

Cromwell soared like an arrow—a plush brown arrow with flapping ears and pointed tail.

This time there was never any question as to whether he would nudge the bottom of the hoop—he cleared it with room to spare, nearly scraping the top.

The crowd gasped again.

Cromwell landed with perfect balance and raced without the slightest hesitation to the finish line, Kevin at his side.

The judges stared at one another, stunned. The entire arena seemed to turn in unison toward the blinking clock:

0:00:39.800.

The judges looked at Kevin, nodding their approval, and the crowd erupted in cheers. Everyone knew there had been no imperfections.

Cameras were flashing all around Kevin and Cromwell.

Elka raced to the judges' table and flung herself at Kevin, hoisting him up briefly—much to his surprise—and then setting him down. She picked up Cromwell, too, hugging him and spinning him around. The dog woofed happily.

"And that is *another* new MKCC record!" declared the P.A. announcer, barely audible over the crowd noise.

Kevin's head swiveled. The scene felt faraway, as if someone else were at its center. People seemed to cheer in slow motion, and voices sounded muffled. The word RECORD blinked on the scoreboard. Kevin noticed that the WFRK reporter—a youngish woman with poofy hair and a thick layer of makeup—had abandoned Shasta and was charging through the crowd toward him.

He was still stunned and out of breath when she arrived.

"That's right, Brad!" she began. "We have breaking news here at the agility show, believe it or not! I'm here with . . . um . . . what's your name, young man?"

The microphone was thrust in Kevin's direction,

and he examined it as though it were a glowing meteor, at first saying nothing.

Elka entered the frame with Cromwell in her arms.

"This amazing young man's name is Kevin Pugh," she said, beaming. "And *this* is his masterful dog, Cromwell, a creature of extraordinary character."

"W-we won?" asked Kevin, still panting.

Cromwell licked his cheek.

"You did, Mr. Pugh," said Elka.

"And in record time!" chirped the reporter.

"Hey, are we on with Brad Ainsworth?" asked Kevin rather dreamily.

"Yes, we are, Kevin. Anything you'd like to say to Brad while we're on the ai—"

"*WHOOOOOOOOO!*" screamed Kevin.

"*WHOOOOOOOOO!*" screamed Zach, chest-bumping his friend, then raising the logo of his Team Cromwell jersey.

"*WHOOOOOOOOO!*"

"As you can see, Brad," the reporter said, attempting to gain control of the conversation, "there's absolute pandemonium here at the United Cen—"

Kevin grabbed the microphone.

"*Champ-ee-uhhhnnnn! WHOOOOOOOO!* Take *that,* Ainsworth! And tell your boy that Kevin Pugh is comin' for him!" Kevin gestured from his eyes to the camera, then back to his eyes. "You got me,

Ainsworth?! You hear me, old man?! I'm talkin' kick-ball, next summer! I will *own* you, Bradley Junior! *WHOOOOOOO . . .*"

The reporter grabbed at the mic as Kevin and Zach hooted.

"I won! I won!"

Kevin wrestled for control of the microphone again, noting the panic in the eyes of the reporter.

"Make me your wacky sports blooper *now,* Ainsworth!"

The petrified reporter finally yanked the microphone back from Kevin's hand. Izzy came pogoing through the live camera shot, searching out Cromwell. A grinning Howie Pugh stepped in front of Kevin and wrapped his arms around him, then squeezed.

"I'm proud of you, kid," he whispered.

"Because I won!" screamed Kevin. "*WHOOO-OOOOO!* I won!"

He leapt onto his dad's wide back, then climbed atop his shoulders and thrust both arms into the air.

"Nah," said Howie. "I'm proud of you because you *tried,* because you gave this thing your best effort and you . . ."

"And I *won*! I can't believe we won!"

Howie grinned, sneaking into the WFRK camera's frame as the reporter struggled to sign off.

Izzy picked up Cromwell and continued hopping. Elka had a preposterously large trophy in her hands.

Kevin stared at the field of handlers and their pampered dogs.

"Is there *no one* to challenge me?!" he yelled.

"I don't think they normally talk a lotta smack at these things, Kev," said Howie. "Maybe you should just . . ."

"WHOOOOOOOOOO!" screamed Kevin, high over his father's head.

Howie grinned. Elka slid past him, patting his shoulder.

"I'm so happy you were here today, Mr. Pugh."

"Me, too." Howie smiled. "Me, too."

"WHOOOOOOOOOO!"

"Ms. Brandt," said Howie. "Do you think the boy is gonna keep entering these competitions?"

She looked up at Kevin. He had taken the trophy from her and was swinging it above his head in a wide arc.

"I would imagine so, yes," said Elka. "He seems rather pleased with himself at the moment. I hope you will approve of Kevin and Cromwell's continued involvement with dog agility train—"

"Oh, yeah," said Howie. "Couldn't be happier. That's not the thing at all."

"What is it, then?"

"Well, if we're going to stick with this stuff . . ."

"WHOOOOOOOOOO!"

". . . at some point we'll have to discuss . . ."

"WHOOOOOOOOOO!"

". . . a few basic principles of sportsmanship."

Elka smiled.

"I quite agree, Mr. Pugh . . ."

"WHOOOOOOOOOO!"

". . . although I do not think . . ."

"WHOOOOOOOOOO!"

". . . the lesson would sink in right now."

27

Kevin leaned back confidently, fluffing a couch cushion with his left hand while leaving his right on the controller. He smirked and stared at the screen.

Left arrow . . . down arrow . . . "X" button . . .

Kevin's smirk widened into a toothy grin.

"This is just too . . ."

His purple-clad receiver hauled in a pass along the left sideline, then high-stepped into the end zone.

". . . easy."

Kevin dropped the controller at his feet and stood up, his palms raised.

"Seriously, that was way too easy. I've always been good, it's true. But it's possible that I've found a new plateau here today."

He stared down at the couch.

"It's 37–0," said Kevin. "Do you seriously want to continue this farce?"

"I-I don't . . ."

Howie Pugh stroked his mustache, his controller in his lap. He wore one of his old jerseys. Howie stared at the TV as if in disbelief.

"You don't have words for the utter *mastery* you've just beheld?" asked Kevin, edging closer to his father. "The timeless dominance? The full expression of my Madden *genius?*"

"Well . . ." began Howie tentatively, "I mean, the Vikings were so bad that year."

"Uh-huh," said Kevin. "My quarterback what's-his-name is like a 76. That really is pretty bad, Dad."

"And the Bears were so *good,*" said Howie, shaking his head.

"Yup, I know. That's why I encouraged you to be Chicago." Kevin rested a hand on his father's shoulder. "If *I* were the Bears and *you* were the Vikings, it would be, like, 72–0 right now."

Howie stared up at his son with a mixture of confusion and stubbornness in his eyes.

"I think maybe this controller is bust—"

"Dad, we've switched controllers eight or nine bazillion times. The gadget is fine. It's operator error."

"Okay, so how did you know I was going to . . . ?"

"Come out of that cover-two? Yeah, that was sweet. If there's one thing Howie Pugh can't stand, it's having his run defense gashed." Kevin imitated a few head fakes; then he mimed a quarterback dropping back to pass. "And I knew I'd get you with the corner-post route. It's my signature play. Don't feel bad, though, because Zach can't stop it, either."

Howie continued to stare at his son, but his expression changed to awestruck pride.

"Yes, Dad, I am intimately familiar with the corner-post. I'm kind of deadly with the screen pass, too, as you've seen. And of course I've got the hitch-and-go for an easy six basically whenever I want it, and . . ."

"All right, rematch. C'mon. I know the beloved Bears aren't going to get shut out, not against the Vikings, of all tea—"

Cromwell leapt onto the couch between them, his leash in his mouth. He woofed once and dropped his leash.

"Gotta go, old man."

Kevin swatted Howie's rounded midsection as he snatched the leash from atop the couch.

"Kev, it's *raining* out there. You can't seriously be thinking about . . ."

"Running?" Kevin looked at his father indignantly. Cromwell seemed to as well.

Howie's glance fell.

"Dad, being a winner is not a part-time commitment," Kevin lectured. "Do you think Shasta and Jody take the afternoon off *when it rains*? I think not."

"Shasta and Jody are probably sticking pins in little Kevin and Cromwell dolls," said Howie. "And then setting them on fire."

Kevin attached the leash to Cromwell's collar.

"Well," he said, "maybe little Kevin Pugh dolls. Not sure about Crom. I felt like maybe there wasn't the same level of animosity between Jody and Cromwell."

"You felt a love connection, maybe?" asked Howie.

Cromwell simply panted excitedly.

Howie perked up. "We should get those two together, Kev. Imagine the puppies! They'd be unstoppable! They'd be masters of agili—"

"Yeesh," said Kevin, stretching in preparation for his run. "It wasn't so long ago that you were *mocking* these dogs, Dad. Now you're envisioning the next generation of agility champions."

"We could be a dynasty, Kev. Like the Bears of Halas, years ago."

Kevin continued to stretch.

"We can't talk dynasty without getting a few more wins under our belt, Dad. You gotta take 'em one competition . . ."

". . . at a time. Yeah, I know. I get paid to dispense such wisdom." Howie straightened, growing more animated as he spoke. "But let's just say Cromwell strings together a few "W's" in the major competitions. Then we need to think of the Pughs as an agility franchise."

"Like we're a NASCAR family? The Earnhardts? Or the Pettys?"

"Exactly! A multi-generational dynasty. That's where the real money is. That's how you get your name on lunch boxes and clothing lines."

"Well," said Kevin, bending forward to touch his toes, "*this* generation needs to get win number three. And we won't get win number three by letting a little rain stop us."

"But, Kev, it could seriously pour out there. The skies could open. How 'bout we just finish the second half of the game here?" Howie turned around slowly to face his son. "You know, the weather guy at WYCR says . . ."

But Kevin was already halfway up the basement steps, Cromwell bounding ahead of him. They reached the top step in full stride, slipped between Maggie and Izzy, and then hit the kitchen door.

Kevin and Cromwell raced down the sidewalk, eyes squinting against the rain. Cromwell's tongue flapped wildly. He leapt a puddle.

"We'll need to finish that course in 38 seconds next time for sure!" shouted Kevin. He sped past a mail carrier, then jumped a hydrant. "Might even need to go 37, because Shasta was *not* a gracious second-place finisher." Kevin leapt over a planting bed with Cromwell at his heels. "See, you've gotta *really* want this, Cromwell, if you're going to defend that champ—"

The dog glanced up, woofed, and locked eyes with Kevin as they ran.

"Okay, so you don't need the pep talks. Me, I sometimes do."

Cromwell barked, dipped his head, and broke into an all-out sprint. Kevin chased after him, grinning, his shoes squishing, the leash held loose in his hand.

Acknowledgments

The author wishes to extend his sincere gratitude to everyone at Alloy Entertainment, and he would like to specifically flatter/thank Sara Shandler, Katie Schwartz, and Josh Bank. Also, many thanks to Nancy Hinkel, Nora Pelizzari, Jan Dundon, Jennifer Boss, Ella Behrens, and All For Doggies Chicago.

Two canines must be acknowledged as well: Izzy and Henry. The latter is a stout pug, fond of sausage. Needs to change his lifestyle. Consider this an intervention, fatty.

About the Author

Andy Behrens is the author of two previous children's books and has written for the *Chicago Reader, Flak Magazine,* and ESPN.com, among others. He lives in Chicago with his wife and daughter and is a self-described "avid, somewhat psychotic Bears fan."